Unusual Fragments

Unusual Fragments

Japanese Stories

CALICO

© 2025 by Two Lines Press

The copyright to the individual pieces in this book remains with the individual authors and translators unless otherwise stated.

"Suna no Ori" by Taeko Kono © 1976 by Akira Kono. English translation rights arranged with Akira Kono through Japan Foreign-Rights Centre.

Unusual Fragments is eleventh in the Calico Series.

Two Lines Press
582 Market Street, Suite 700, San Francisco, CA 94104
www.twolinespress.com

ISBN: 978-1-949641-75-2

Cover design by Crisis
Cover image © Masahisa Fukase Archives
Typesetting and interior design by Marie-Noëlle Hébert
Printed in the United States of America

Library of Congress Cataloging-in-Publication Data available upon request.

THIS BOOK WAS PUBLISHED WITH SUPPORT
FROM THE NATIONAL ENDOWMENT FOR THE ARTS

The Hole in the Sky
NOBUKO TAKAGI, translated by Philip Price
9

Husband in a Box
TOMOKO YOSHIDA, translated by Margaret Mitsutani
37

The False Mustache
TARUHO INAGAKI, translated by Jeffrey Angles
67

Hot Day
TAKAKO TAKAHASHI, translated by Brian Bergstrom
85

Cage of Sand
TAEKO KONO, translated by Lucy North
111

Contributors
157

天の穴

The Hole in the Sky

Nobuko Takagi

Translated by Philip Price

The Hole in the Sky

Toyoko squinted past the moving windshield wipers to the blackness beyond. The rain seemed to have stopped to catch its breath.

It was always this way in a typhoon: the capricious sky would suddenly spit out huge drops of rain, and then pause for a second to see the effect it was having on those down below. Then, when everyone had let down their guard, it would hurl down those huge rain drops again, but this time diagonally and right into its victims' faces.

Toyoko could do nothing in the face of these spasmodic attacks but grip the steering wheel and let out a snort of contempt. Her day had been filled with such unpleasant incidents, all of them unexpected. According to the weather forecast, the typhoon was supposed to reach the southern tip of Kyushu tomorrow afternoon and then make its way along the coastline to Shikoku. Instead, it had suddenly accelerated and shifted northward until it blasted straight into Fukuoka, the city where Toyoko lived. Of course, typhoons had a habit of doing these things, and there was nothing anyone could do about it, yet today's unexpected weather had gone and knocked everything off course.

During her lunch break, Toyoko had left the admin building of the university where she worked and walked through the pine grove to the road to buy some lunch. As she thought about it later, she realized she should have made do with a boxed lunch from the Agricultural Department next door, but instead she had decided she wanted to walk in the rain, just to be different from everyone else. Once again, the blame lay with the typhoon.

At the entrance to an old-fashioned post office on the other side of the zebra crossing, she saw a fat little old woman carrying a paper bag. Unprotected by the woman's umbrella, the bag had been soaked through and burst open, spilling its contents onto the concrete steps leading up to the post office door. Toyoko looked down and saw three ripe mangoes—the yellow type from the Philippines—rolling around in the rain. The old woman was just standing there staring calmly down at her feet, so Toyoko reluctantly crossed the street, picked up the mangoes, and handed them to their owner. If they had been anything other than mangoes, she would perhaps have shown a little more kindness and concern.

The combination of the silly old woman and her mangoes in the pouring rain of the approaching typhoon made Toyoko feel sick, as if she had seen a middle-aged man with his arm around a teenage girl's waist. For Toyoko, a mango was a sophisticated, stylish fruit, more suited to a chic young woman.

The old woman took the mangoes from her and held them against her chest, muttering, "Oh, the poor things, they're all bruised." She didn't bother to look at the face of the considerate lady who had picked them up for her. Toyoko's fingers stank of mango juice. In fact, the woman had whispered some words of thanks, but Toyoko hadn't heard them; she had already turned and begun to walk briskly away. Just as she was stepping onto the sidewalk from the zebra crossing, she fell and twisted her right ankle.

Later that afternoon, Toyoko's husband called from his office in Osaka to say that he wouldn't be able to make it home that weekend. It wasn't the first time this had happened. Before he could provide an excuse, Toyoko threw him a lifeline, saying, "Well, the typhoon's coming after all."

"Right, the trains probably won't be running," added her husband, sounding relieved.

After she had replaced the receiver, she became angry with herself, wondering why on earth she had let him off the hook so easily. Countless times throughout her unremarkable forty-five years of life she had thrown someone a lifeline while giving herself up to the waves, and here she was doing the same thing with her husband. She should have listened to his excuses, even if she knew they were lies.

There were several other incidents throughout the day that had annoyed her. She could simply have put it down to the typhoon, but Toyoko always felt that when something irritating or unexpected occurred, she was somehow responsible.

The wind was growing stronger by the minute. The wipers worked frantically to clear the windshield in front of Toyoko's eyes.

Her colleagues had all gone home early, but Toyoko had stayed at her desk longer than usual, partly because her husband wasn't coming home, and partly through a sense of defiance, as if to say, "So what? It's only a typhoon." So she couldn't really complain about the rainstorm that was raging around her now as she drove.

Toyoko often found herself doing things that were pointlessly stubborn. Near her childhood home there had been a graveyard, and even though it wasn't any quicker, she would force herself to walk through it at night. And yet, whenever the topic came up with her friends and parents, she would open her eyes wide in fright and swear she could never bring herself to do just that. Standing still in the middle of the graveyard, she would stare at the gravestones lined up in the dark, sensing a presence. She knew there was something there, but she was also certain that the key to saving herself from being sucked in was to call out to it, urging it to suck her in if it dared. Her actions were less a sign of courage than of childish belligerence, but on those nights in the graveyard she would feel a power surge within her at the thought that there was a whole side of her that her family didn't know existed.

This is how Toyoko had lived her life: blasting her way through the unknown while everyone else just hoped to pass by unnoticed, always throwing the first punch to protect herself from injury. In this way she had come to feel a secret sense of superiority, although a stranger would probably find it difficult to see her as anything other than the typical dog in the manger: grudging, headstrong, and obstinate. And she knew that most people thought of her in exactly those terms.

In the early years of her marriage, her husband had often urged her to be more open, but she had no idea how and became angry, feeling that she was being unfairly criticized. She realized then that if she admitted to her failings, even to her husband, she would leave herself vulnerable to attack and end up being eaten away from the inside out. So she told her husband not to even think about trying to change her. From then on, she knew that, for no particular reason, she would never be a happy woman. And yet she had always believed that even without happiness, she would find a way to lead a determined, powerful life.

The stoplight turned green.

The moment she pressed her foot on the accelerator, her car was pelted by rain coming down like a waterfall from above the lights. She saw a dark shadow through the wall of water and slammed on the brakes. In an instant her whole body was covered in a cold sweat. It didn't seem as if the car had collided with anything, and there had been no loud noise, so what was the dark shadow?

She pulled on the parking brake and peered out beyond the wipers at the pedestrian crossing. Any light that gathered on the windshield was soon wiped away, making it impossible to get a good look at the scene in front of her. When another car passed by without showing any particular interest, she calmed down, thinking that nothing terrible could have happened.

Just as she was about to release the parking brake, a human figure emerged in the lower-left corner of the windshield. It appeared to be a child. Toyoko leaped out of the driving seat and felt a jolt of pain running through the ankle she had twisted earlier that afternoon. She waded through the beams of her headlights, dragging her twisted ankle behind her as she ran.

"Hey! Hey you! Are you OK?"

It was a boy. Having no children of her own, she couldn't tell how old he was, but somehow he seemed both too big to be in elementary school and too small for junior high. He wore a baseball cap pulled down low over his forehead, long pants, and a short-sleeved shirt. His whole body was dripping wet, as if he had just climbed out of the ocean.

"Are you hurt? Did I hit you?"

It was too dark to see his face. His baseball cap looked as if it was about to be knocked to the ground by the driving rain. She grabbed his hand and was surprised by its size and strength, but even in the warm night air it was shaking and stiff.

"Well, I suppose you'd better get in."

The boy climbed into the front passenger seat without protest, and immediately the car was filled with a strange odor, fishy and sweet-sour.

Toyoko looked at the boy's profile. The dim light dappled his nose and cheeks, making it impossible to get a good look at him; one moment he looked like a young man, and the next like a small child. Despite his short stature, he appeared grown up, and his face was large.

"Are you hurt anywhere?"

He twisted his upper body around to face her in the driver's seat. Toyoko flinched, but when she noticed that his head just barely came up to her neck, she relaxed. He was only a child after all.

"You just fell down, right? That's all?"

The boy said "Yes" in such a deep, loud voice that Toyoko jumped.

"What kind of boy speaks in *that* voice?" she thought. She began to feel a little weak.

"You gave me such a shock! I thought I'd run someone over. I'll drive you home."

Cars were coming up behind them and speeding past one after another. She was worried that one of them would drive straight into them.

"Fasten your seatbelt."

The boy did as he was told.

"What are you doing without an umbrella? There's a typhoon coming you know. And what were you doing there anyway, getting in my way like that?"

Having assured herself that the boy wasn't injured, Toyoko became irritated. She would never have been burdened with this unwanted passenger if he hadn't been a child.

Toyoko was not a tolerant woman, and she had no love for children. She often thought that if she'd had children of her own, she would have become one of those mothers whose children despise them, and so she had never longed for motherhood. Besides, relations with her husband had cooled long ago. She neither loved her husband nor enjoyed her work. Sometimes she was revolted by her own unpleasantness.

She had felt a huge sense of relief when she realized that the boy was unharmed, but after driving through three green lights and stopping at the next red, she cursed the ceaseless rain for dragging her into yet another annoying situation.

"The typhoon will pass through here in around thirty minutes," said the boy in a monotone voice.

"Thirty minutes? Who told you that?"

"They said so on TV."

Toyoko hadn't heard any news about the typhoon in her office and was vaguely dismayed to learn that it was so close. If the typhoon was only thirty minutes away, the wind and rain would be at their peak right about now.

"But a typhoon is big. It's hundreds of kilometers across. It doesn't just pass through in thirty minutes or twenty minutes like a train, you know."

"Well, that depends on the typhoon. This typhoon has an extremely large eye. The position of the eye has been identified clearly from the weather station. Reports are coming in rapidly on the internet."

Toyoko was caught off guard by grown-up words such as "identified" and "rapidly" coming with such assurance and precision from the mouth of this boy who looked like a drowned rat, and while waiting at the next red light, her feelings toward him turned to pure dislike. "What a nasty little boy with his big words and big head," she thought. He reminded her of one of those kids who murder their parents without a second thought. Sometimes they would publish the diaries of those kids in the papers, and they always sounded as if they'd been written by an adult.

Toyoko turned to look at the front passenger seat. The boy was staring straight ahead, silent and unblinking. His back was so straight it seemed as though he wasn't even breathing. She began devising how and where to chase this little pest out of her car, and quickly realized the difficulty of the task. He wasn't carrying an umbrella or a bag, and his feet were covered in nothing but flimsy canvas tennis shoes. The only thing shielding him from the rain was his baseball cap. There was no way she could fling him out into the wind and rain dressed like that. She decided to stop at the nearest convenience store and drop him off there.

"So I'll just drop you near your house, OK? Or if there's a convenience store nearby I can stop there if you want."

The boy's profile clouded over, but the nape of his neck stood as straight as the stalk of a plant and his cheeks remained firm.

"The eye of this particular typhoon is believed to have a diameter of around ten kilometers."

"Oh, I see."

Toyoko searched desperately for a convenience store on the road ahead. She had already found one, but the lights had been off, presumably because of the typhoon. A while back she had passed a gas station, but no one had been there and the entrance had been blocked by a chain.

"Ten kilometers is comparatively small. Big ones can be up to a hundred kilometers. When the eye is formed, the atmospheric pressure at the center begins to fall rapidly, and as the typhoon develops, the size of the eye decreases. In a powerful typhoon, it's either square or pentagonal or hexagonal."

"What is?"

"The eye."

"Hexagonal?"

"It depends on the pressure-gradient force, centrifugal force, Coriolis force, and also friction with the surface of the earth and the sea."

Toyoko began to feel a slight pain in her chest. The boy remained perfectly still.

"…if we assume that the Coriolis parameter is f and the wind velocity is v, then the magnitude of the Coriolis force can be expressed as fv. And if we calculate the angular velocity of the earth rate as a, the Coriolis factor…"

"Where do they come from?"

"Where do what come from?"

"Typhoons. Where do they come from?"

"It depends on the season."

"What about this one?"

"Well, usually at this time of year typhoons are generated in the ocean east of the Philippines between longitude 120 and 140 degrees east, but this one actually developed into a typhoon from a westward tropical cyclone after it passed into the Sulu Sea from the Philippine Sea."

"And then it came all the way to Fukuoka?"

"It's actually an extremely rare case."

"What's its name?"

"Number 21."

"And what's your name?"

"I thought we were talking about the typhoon."

"Look, if you won't tell me your name, I'm going to drop you off right here, OK?"

The boy pulled the brim of his baseball cap down to his nose so that only his thick lips caught the dim light of the evening. He had cunning, leering lips that again belied his age.

Toyoko checked that there were no cars behind her and lifted her foot. Just as she was about to step on the brake, the lips began to move.

"...I would very much like to see the eye of the typhoon. It's really close, and I've been waiting for so many years."

His voice had suddenly become weak and pleading. Toyoko moved her foot away from the brake and pounded the steering wheel angrily with her hand.

"So where the hell is this eye, then?"

"If you stop the car I'll find it for you."

She stopped the car, assuming the boy would jump out and run off, but instead he lifted his baseball cap and peered intently out into the darkness.

"Which way is the wind blowing now?" he asked.

"Oh, it's just coming from all over the place, isn't it," replied Toyoko.

"If you look at that tree, you'll be able to tell. It's coming in at an angle from the rear left. If the typhoon starts to move south, we'll be too late, but if we go now, we should be able to make it. The eye of the typhoon is right over there. Look, over there!"

Toyoko followed his finger to a flashing neon sign on a building to their right. The weakness in his voice had disappeared and he seemed to be brimming with confidence again. He had the dense eyebrows and sunken cheeks of a philosopher, but his neck and shoulders were scrawny and childlike. It was like discovering a new species of mammal with a bizarrely unbalanced body.

The Hole in the Sky

Toyoko suddenly felt the surge of an emotion she had not experienced since she'd stood in the middle of the graveyard as a child. Running away now would mean defeat, and so she resolved to stay the course, no matter what. And if they couldn't find the eye of the typhoon where he said it would be, she would deal with him appropriately.

They were silent all the way to Momochi Beach. Now and again the boy would hitch himself forward and point the way through the darkness with his index finger, paying no attention whatsoever to roads, stoplights, or street corners.

The parking lot was empty.

"Well, we can't go any farther, unless we drive right into the ocean. So where's this eye of yours?"

Again the boy shrank into the passenger seat. He looked timidly out to sea, but there was nothing but blackness.

"Why don't you get out and go take a look?" Toyoko suggested, figuring she could get rid of him.

The driving rain had eased a little, indicating that they had entered a trough of the typhoon, but still it showed no signs of stopping. The boy sat motionlessly, focusing doggedly on the view through the windshield.

"It won't be long now," he said. "In a few minutes the rain will stop, and then we'll enter the eye."

"That's all very well and good," thought Toyoko, "but what's so special about the eye of a typhoon anyway?"

Toyoko held no fear of the unknown—she had overcome that particular emotion long ago in the graveyard of her childhood—but when the rain stopped falling and the wind stopped blowing precisely five minutes later, she couldn't help but feel somewhat disconcerted.

The boy gripped the brim of his baseball cap and pulled it down over his face, then opened the car door and got out. Toyoko watched apprehensively as he passed through the beams of the headlights, climbed down the tree-lined steps, and disappeared, seemingly oblivious to the peculiarity of the whole situation. He had jumped out of the car energetically, but now he limped gingerly down the steps like an old man, his right shoulder sagging.

Toyoko decided to wait a while, but when he hadn't returned after ten minutes or so, she turned off the engine, checked that the wind and rain hadn't started up again, and got out of the car. She walked over to the steps and stood at the top. She had been to this beach once before, many years ago. She recalled that the fenced parking lot led down to a grove of pine trees, and beyond the trees the beach stretched out endlessly in either direction. But now Toyoko was faced with nothing but a dark void. She managed to make out the boundary between the sea and sand from the different shades of gray.

Faint white lights flickered now and then like writhing snakes as waves crashed to shore.

"Hey! Hey you!" she called out, and soon a reply came from the sand dunes nearby. She clambered through the darkness toward the voice, and once she figured she was close enough, she sat down, feeling that if she remained standing, he would suddenly appear from nowhere and scare her. As the last gasps of wind blew down from high up in the sky, the sound of the roaring waves seemed to grow louder.

"Has the eye arrived? It seems to have arrived, don't you think?" Not really knowing why—perhaps because of the sheer blackness of the night—Toyoko felt she ought to speak to the boy a little more respectfully than before.

"It's heading right toward us. It should be here in just a few minutes. It's moving along the boundary between land and sea, though, so there's some variation in the frictional force. If the centrifugal force or the wind velocity changes even slightly, the temperature of the air that gets sucked into the center of the eye decreases, and that leads to a decrease in the amount of water vapor. So it's probably going to be five or ten minutes late."

"But we're right in the middle of the eye now, aren't we? The rain and wind have stopped."

"Well, meteorologically speaking that's true, but there has

to be a hole for us to be truly in the center of the eye. There has to be a hole…"

The gloom enveloping the boy's body seemed to grow even denser, leaving only his hurried breathing perceptible.

"So will we be able to see this hole? Is it big?"

"The eye of this typhoon is very peculiar. I don't suppose you've ever seen a sectional diagram of the eye of a typhoon, have you? The eye is surrounded by a wall of cloud up to fifteen kilometers high. The clouds spin round, creating an incredibly powerful upward current, and then they spread out at the top like the cap of a mushroom. Lots of things are carried on the mushroom cap, like fish and leaves that have been sucked up by the eye. Heavy things fall through, but anything lightweight gets carried along by the clouds, similarly to a plastic ball bouncing around at the top of a fountain."

"Did you learn all this on your own?"

"I've got lots of books under my bed. The old ones are too easy for me now though, so I suppose I should donate them to a public library or something. And then of course there's the internet. NASA has the best site for the latest information."

"So how old are you, anyway? And don't lie to me, OK?"

"I don't see what my age has got to do with anything. Hyades is around 500 million years old. Pleiades was born

The Hole in the Sky

20 million years ago at least. Of course you're more likely to know Pleiades as Subaru."

His voice gradually grew quieter as he spoke.

"Fine, so you won't tell me your name and you won't tell me how old you are. No problem. But you must have parents somewhere?"

"There's just Granddad and me."

Finally, he had spoken like a child.

"Ah, so I guess your granddad is a fan of typhoons too, right?"

"He had a friend who he thought had died on Leyte Island during the war, but this friend was carried back to Japan by a typhoon and dropped through the hole in the eye. He twisted his ankle when he fell, but after that he got married and lived for another twenty years. In 1949 the eye of another typhoon passed right over my granddad's head, and he said that when he looked up, he could see Pleiades clearly through the hole in the eye."

"Gosh, I'd pay a lot of money to meet the man who fell through the typhoon," said Toyoko.

"He's dead so you can't. The upward current in the wall of the eye is incredibly powerful, but in the center of the eye it reverses and hot, dry air comes pouring down. Would you like me to explain how the flow of air switches from the wall to the center?"

"No thanks, I think I can live without another explanation. So you're waiting for someone to come falling through the eye, right?"

"Yes."

"Another friend who died in the war, perhaps?"

"I don't have any friends."

"Who, then?"

"My mother."

"Is she dead too?"

The boy paused for a long time, and then replied, "Yes, she's dead too."

"Did she die in the Philippines?"

"I guess so. She went back there."

"But we can't just have your mother falling through the sky, can we? Your father will have to come with her."

"I never had a father."

"OK, so you had a mother and then she went away and now she's dead. Am I correct so far?"

Toyoko realized that she was displaying another of her bad habits—mocking people by throwing their words back at them. She was becoming more and more infuriated and longed for the rain to start falling again so she could get the hell out of there. But the boy fell silent, leaving only the endless crashing of the waves to be heard.

The Hole in the Sky

"So where's this granddad of yours then?"

"I don't know. I haven't seen him for a long time."

"Well, is he dead or alive?"

"He's dead, of course."

"Of course!" thought Toyoko. "How could I be so stupid?"

"So everyone is dead, and you're the only one left alive."

"Yes. But soon they're all going to come falling through the hole. Very soon."

The sky remained dark, and Toyoko could see nothing that resembled the eye of a typhoon. She felt trapped, as if enclosed in a red-hot capsule. She began to sweat and felt her chest break out in goosebumps.

"...it must have passed by," whispered Toyoko, but as she spoke, she sensed that the boy had stood up. His black shadow loomed monstrously over her as she crouched on the sand.

"There it is! Can't you see it? Look! There!"

He began running toward the sea's edge. Toyoko stood up and chased after his shadow. She heard a loud splash as he jumped into the water and realized that the tide had come in fast while they'd been talking. From the coughing sound that followed she guessed he must have fallen and swallowed seawater. She could easily have run into the waves and helped him up, but instead she stopped at the sand's edge. It wouldn't be the greatest tragedy the world had ever known if he were to drown.

If that was what fate had in store for him, then so be it. As she listened attentively to his coughing, she felt she was back in her graveyard. She knew there was something in there, but she wasn't scared. Nobody knew how brave she was, but *she* knew.

The boy crawled out of the gray foam, landed at her feet, and grabbed her right ankle. She was overwhelmed by the touch of his hand, so soft and warm that she felt her leg might melt away. She looked up and saw the eye of the typhoon.

As the boy continued wheezing on the sand beside her, desperately trying to catch his breath, she sat down and hugged her knees to her chest. The boy kept hold of her right ankle, which was still a little swollen from when she had twisted it earlier that day, and together they looked up at the sky.

"We've found it at last! See those jagged edges? That's the wall of cloud. It's quite high, probably fifteen kilometers, like a long tunnel. And then that thin layer at the top of the wall is cirrus cloud. It'll move away in a minute and the hole will open up. Watch carefully. See? It's moving, can you tell? The eye is searching for me. Look, it's getting bigger! Longitude 130 east, 50 minutes... No, more precisely... Oh, I can't remember! Latitude 438 north, 29 minutes, 8 seconds... In terms of right ascension and declination... Today is the fifty-fifth day of the first month, so the right ascension is 10h 35m and the declination is +22 degrees... Look! There's the eye, just where

I said it would be. It's opened right up! You can see the stars through it. Oh, I wish I'd brought my cosmological time chart with me."

"What stars are they?" asked Toyoko, her eyes closed.

"Um, one moment… Yes, M81 and M82. They're part of the Great Bear. There's no way you'd ever be able to see them from my bedroom. My bedroom faces southwest, so I can only see a quarter of the universe. Look, there's M97! It's a perfect circle, just like a planet, although strictly speaking it's a nebula, of course. It's almost as bright as the spiral Andromeda Galaxy, but its shape is completely different. My granddad said we shouldn't call Andromeda a spiral galaxy because really it's an elliptical galaxy. It's not quite as bright as Andromeda, but it's so beautiful. I've got my own here. This is *my* elliptical Andromeda Galaxy."

The boy took Toyoko's hands in his and placed them on his head. She guessed his baseball cap must have been washed away by the waves, for her fingers came into contact with a warm, wet, clean-shaven scalp. As she explored her way over the boy's head, she found a soft part that was smooth and slippery like the skin of a fruit. Every time she tried to move away from it, he guided her fingers back there, forcing her to touch it again and again. It was so soft she felt that if she were to press down, her fingers would leave deep indentations, or even break through to the liquid beneath. Slowly she began to enjoy the tender sensation in her fingers, and before long she was unable to move her hand away.

"There's no bone here," she whispered. She looked up through the wild, ghostly pine trees to the boundless sky, lit up by a single, elliptical star hanging low as if resting just above them.

"Yes, I can see it. The elliptical Andromeda Galaxy." As she spoke, her fingers continued to investigate the contours of his head. Whenever she tried to stop them moving, she felt a strange power surge through her shoulders, forcing her to press down hard onto his soft scalp, and again she was afraid she would break through. The texture reminded her of the mangoes she had picked up for the old lady earlier that day.

"It smells so good," said the boy. Toyoko had noticed it too: a sweet odor emanating from the boy's body, more precisely from his head. She lifted her hands and pressed them to her nose: the fragrance of the afternoon's mangoes seeped through her nostrils.

"See? I told you so," he purred in a gentle, childish voice.

"What did you tell me?"

"That someone would fall through the eye of the typhoon."

Toyoko nodded her head. Sure enough she felt that a brand new version of herself had fallen upon her.

The Hole in the Sky

For a while the two of them remained seated on the sand, staring up at the sky and talking in disjointed sentences that, if anyone had been listening, must have sounded like some kind of alien language.

"So I've been reborn," said Toyoko.

"My skull was broken into eight pieces, but your head was smaller than mine, so it smashed into tiny fragments," explained the boy.

"It happened in the afternoon, right?"

"No, it was early evening. The typhoon lifted the car right up along the clouds and then spat it out through the hole."

"Yes. Now I remember. It was early evening, and the typhoon was coming closer and closer, so quickly…"

And for all those years afterward I was just floating around in the sky, sometimes as M97, sometimes as *a* or *b*, then as one of the stars on the Great Bear's tail, and then as Hercules' foot.

A moist, warm wind suddenly blew up, and before long rain started to fall again. Toyoko grabbed the boy's hand and they ran to the car. The raindrops began to swell, becoming more voluminous as they bounced off the windshield.

They drove back along the same roads, and when they arrived at the lights where Toyoko had first picked the boy up, she turned to face the front passenger seat and asked him where he would like to be dropped off. As before, he gave her directions until they came to a large palm tree by the side of the road with a sagging branch.

"Stop here," he said quietly.

Ahead of them stood a large square building, a hospital, with a blue neon cross attached to the wall.

"See you, then," said Toyoko.

The boy gave Toyoko a brief sideways glance, got out of the car silently, and walked away without looking back. Toyoko knew she would never set eyes on him again. She guessed she would miss him terribly for the next few days, his strange scent and the sensation of his head on her fingertips. She imagined how she would long to see him whenever a typhoon blew up on a summer evening, so much that her chest would hurt, and yet she knew she would never find him, that she would simply have to withstand the pain.

She watched the boy walk until his outline was blurred by the rain. The hospital was surrounded by a jumble of old houses, and it was impossible to tell which building he had entered. She decided that he had gone back to the psychiatric ward of the hospital. Choosing such a poignant fate for him made her feel somehow at peace; she couldn't bear the thought that the events of the evening and all the strange things they had talked about had been nothing but a prank played by a boy with an overactive imagination, and so she told herself that

The Hole in the Sky

the damage to his skull had been accompanied by internal damage to his brain.

She paused, perplexed at these new emotions, and rested her head gently in the palm of her left hand. She couldn't help but feel that a hole had opened up somewhere in her, too.

箱の夫

Husband in a Box

Tomoko Yoshida

Translated by Margaret Mitsutani

Husband in a Box

"Are the loquats ripe?" my husband asked at the breakfast table. My mother-in-law ate most of them. She always let us have the first one, though, to share. It was a sort of ritual to mark the beginning of summer.

"Not yet," she said. "Not until after the rainy season." My husband looked out at the garden. "You don't really like loquats anyway," she added. "If you want some, you can have Yasuko buy them at the supermarket."

She looked over at me. I nodded and said, "Of course."

"Nah, no need," he said, reaching for a newspaper clipping. I quickly got up to wipe off the kitchen table and clear away the breakfast dishes.

We had a fig tree, too. I don't understand why, but I've heard people say that loquat and fig trees bring bad luck, so you mustn't have them in your garden. I once asked my mother-in-law if she had planted the trees on purpose. "Well, I guess someone must have," she replied. "Or maybe they just grew on their own." Either way, she didn't seem to care. She never pruned or even mentioned them, but she was always happy to eat the fruit when it was ripe. The figs were large, and very sweet. The loquats had such big seeds they were hardly worth the trouble.

I could see the loquat tree from the kitchen window. It looked weak and spindly, considering how old it was. The branches with fruit on them were kind of creepy, covered with white fuzz. Some tree disease, maybe. The fig tree was on the western side, by my mother-in-law's room, so I hardly ever saw it. But every time I went out to weed the garden, I was startled at how overgrown the branches were. There was something ferocious about the way they covered the entire western garden, four yards wide, and even seemed to be reaching over the fence into the neighbor's yard. I thought it might be better to prune them, but never actually said so. It wasn't a serious problem, and besides, the garden was my mother-in-law's territory.

"Yasuko! Yasuko! Come here!" she shrieked. Wiping my hands on my apron, I rushed into the living room. She was leaning out into the corridor, jabbing one finger toward the yard. A yellow stray cat I'd seen before was on the veranda again. Small for a tom, with a timid little face. "Quick! Chase it away!" my mother-in-law screamed. She loathes cats. My husband once got into a fight with one and was badly hurt, she said, so maybe that's where it started. But how could my mild-mannered husband, who hardly ever spoke, do battle with a cat? Just thinking about it made me laugh. The cat peered into the room, meowed once, then lifted his tail and sprayed the screen door. I opened it and shooed him away. He slowly dropped down onto the grass, then turned back to look at me. "Go on, get out!" I said sternly, intentionally raising my voice. Finally, I threw a stone at him, and he ran off.

"How did that happen?" my mother-in-law demanded to know. "Where did he get in? I put up a net, you know." Her chest was heaving. She seemed genuinely terrified.

"A cat could've easily jumped over that bamboo fence," I said, "even with a net over it."

"Then we'll have to find a dome-shaped one, big enough to cover the whole house," she replied, perfectly serious.

"Yes, it'll have to be really huge," I said. Actually, it would only need to cover my husband. My mother-in-law certainly wasn't going to be devoured by a cat. I got a rag to wipe the screen door, then went back to the kitchen. I heard faint strains of music. Bach seemed to be my husband's favorite composer. He listened to cassette tapes with the sound turned down low. At that volume, you couldn't really hear it, but he never turned it up. Since I liked it too, I made excuses to go into his study whenever he had it on. His study was really the living room, but when we weren't eating or watching TV there, that was where he worked. I usually tried to stay away so as not to disturb him. My mother-in-law had apparently retreated to her room. She used to watch TV there, or, being an early riser, she'd sometimes take a nap. Every morning she was up at five, poring over four different newspapers, stopping to carefully cut out articles on politics, social issues, the stock market, new products or companies, plus a few human-interest stories. My husband read them after breakfast. They were all different sizes, but he nimbly picked each one up with his long, black fingernails. After perusing them he would turn to his computer in the corner where he received information from various companies and sent out messages.

After I'd dried the clean teacups and put them away, I got my husband's water ready. He didn't drink tea or ice water, and since he hated the taste of tap water, I bought purified water, especially for him. He had his own little cup, which I filled exactly 80% full; then, once I'd made sure there were no water droplets clinging to the outside, and that the tray was perfectly dry, I'd take it in to him.

"The weather's so nice today," I said. "I'd like to do the laundry, but is it going to rain?" The weather forecast was never among the articles my mother-in-law cut out of the newspaper, yet even though he didn't watch the weather report on TV either, my husband's predictions were always correct. Peering through his glasses, low down on his nose, his small black eyes surveyed the garden, then looked over at me.

"There'll be a shower this evening," he said.

"If I hang the clothes out now, they'll be dry by then," I said. He nodded, then took an envelope out of a desk drawer and handed it to me. Inside was one opera ticket.

"Oh, *The Magic Flute!*" I cried. I'd seen the newspaper ad, which I'd cut out and slipped into his usual pile of clippings. But that had been about five months ago, so I'd forgotten all about it.

"I've been dying to go. You bought me this ticket? I can go, can't I—this ticket's mine?" I was so happy I was dancing around, waving the ticket in the air. Then I checked the date.

"It's tonight! I'm so excited. One of the best seats, too—this feels like a dream. How can I ever thank you!"

Seeing how thrilled I was, he seemed to be laughing. He opened his mouth so wide I saw red inside. I heard him say something.

"We'll go together."

"Together? But there's only one ticket."

"Doesn't matter."

"By that do you mean you're going with me?"

He said nothing. Which meant I was right. I was so surprised I could hardly breathe. I had never seen him leave the house, not even once.

"Are you sure you can go? Does Mother know about this? How will we get there?"

"We'll leave at six." He then turned back to the computer and started punching keys again.

This was no time to be doing laundry. What would I wear? We'd have to have dinner early. More than that, *how* would he come with me? Why had he bought only one ticket?

But he was definitely going. With me. Just thinking about it made me happy. A real opera, with my real husband. To see *The Magic Flute*. This one opera would be enough to last a lifetime. An opera I'd always dreamed of seeing. I was sure he hadn't bought just the one ticket out of stinginess. He wanted to go with me as one, body and soul. And even if he'd bought two tickets, getting there and coming home would still be a problem. When it came to moving, he was very slow. He was apparently much faster if he used his hands, but he couldn't very well scurry along to the concert hall on all fours. I'd never actually seen him move that way. One day several months before, I'd gone to the supermarket while my mother-in-law was out at her lesson in Noh chanting. When I came home, I went around to the garden to pick some *shiso* leaves for dinner before going inside and saw something moving under the big cherry tree in the southwest corner. At first I thought it was a large mouse, or maybe a small dog. Then it scampered across the garden, up over the veranda, and into the living room. A distance of about eight yards, but the creature crossed it in no time. It seemed to be jumping, above the ground, rather than crawling. I picked up my shopping bag and hurried into the living room to find my husband in his usual position, not the slightest bit out of breath.

"Did you see something come in here?" I asked.

"No," he replied, his back turned.

I went around to face him. "Are you sure?" I asked suspiciously. He was avoiding looking me in the eye, yet the muscles in his face were quivering. Not in anger, though—he seemed to be trying not to laugh. His shoulders were moving slightly, up and down. He then waved me away, so I didn't press the matter. But I'm sure it was him.

There was so much to do. I'd have to wash at least half the dirty clothes that had piled up during this string of rainy days. I'd pick out something to wear tonight while the washing machine was running. My matching skirt and short-sleeved blouse with the little yellow flowers would go nicely with the new Josette summer coat I hadn't worn yet. I might need a wrap if it was chilly in the concert hall. My husband had bought me the coat online. As usual, I'd slipped the order form into his pile of newspaper clippings. Though he never went out, he could apparently purchase whatever he wanted online. The only things he left for me to buy were his purified water, eggplants, seasonings, and plastic garbage bags. A big sack of rice was suddenly delivered to our house once, straight from the farm, along with a big metal washtub. Ordered by my husband, apparently, though he hadn't told anyone. He must have overheard my mother-in-law and me talking about how beaten up our old washtub was. I don't really understand how it works, but it seems he pays for these things by computer, too.

While I was hanging out the wash, my mother-in-law came to help. As she was only about four and a half feet tall, she took charge of the lower pole, while I slung towels and futon covers over the higher one.

"It must be convenient, being so tall," she said. "Big people are born for physical labor. Don't have to use their brains, so they have an easy time of it. For generations, they've called us the Noble One-Foot Wiod Clan. We've always used our heads rather than our bodies."

"Ah," I answered vaguely, wondering what Wiod could mean.

"In families with lots of children," she went on, "it wasn't the firstborn, but the smallest, who was the heir. You could tell at a glance who was the chosen one, the best of the lot. The bigger kids—like me—were given lots of chores from early childhood. I did all kinds of work. I was pushed out because I was too big to inherit, but now I've got my son to care for. Of all the Wiods, there hasn't been as fine a one for a hundred years. We'll have to go to Bakinu sometime soon. The last time I was there, he was just a child, so no one knew yet how well he'd turn out."

I wondered where Bakinu could be. I'd heard her mention it before. She'd talked about going there soon then, too. She looked over at me. "Yes, let's," I blurted out, then started to tell her about tonight's opera.

"We'll be leaving at six," I said, "so I'd like to have dinner an hour earlier than usual. Will that be all right?"

Opening her eyes wide, she stared at me, then said, "The two of you—well, well. An opera—my, my. And leaving at six—my oh my oh my."

Her *well, wells* and *my oh mys* didn't reveal whether she approved or disapproved. They were no help at all. I wished she'd get angry, or object, and then help me come up with some kind of plan. In the past few decades, she must have had to take my husband out somewhere at least once or twice. How, exactly, had she managed it?

"So, uh, what should I do?"

After beating one of my husband's shirts to get the wrinkles out, my mother-in-law hung it on the bamboo pole. She shot a glance at me, then turned and went back into the house. I couldn't tell whether or not she was upset.

When I'd finished with the laundry, I suddenly remembered it was time for lunch. With all the fuss about the opera, it had completely slipped my mind. Though I wasn't hungry at all, I couldn't very well skip it. After all, it was my job to fix our meals.

I boiled some cold *somen* noodles, then took a kitchen knife and chopped them into little pieces the size of rice grains. My husband couldn't swallow long noodles. I cut tiny squares of cucumber and tomato and mixed them with lettuce. He likes food without seasoning—salad vegetables with no salt or mayonnaise, steak so rare it's practically raw, or fish that actually is raw. In other words, he likes his food untreated, just as it is. For dinner I boiled some New Zealand spinach in the water left over from the noodles, washed the rice, and made little chicken mince dumplings rolled in sliced almonds, ready to be fried; then I put them in the refrigerator. While my hands were moving, I worked out a plan. I'd have to take him either in a *furoshiki* wrapping cloth, a basket, or a box. He'd be awfully cramped in a furoshiki, and a basket would be too bulky to take into the concert hall. There'd be no place for a seat inside it, either. A box wrapped in a furoshiki wouldn't attract so much attention, and he'd be able to sit down inside it. He wouldn't be able to stand up or lie down, but everybody sits during operas. No one watches standing up or lying on the floor. Did we have a box that was just the right size? I thought over the various boxes we had in the house. But no, first I'd have to check to see how big it needed to be. I stopped what I was doing, went into my husband's study, and measured him with my eyes. I thought I was being very quiet, but he noticed and turned around. Seeing I was emptyhanded, he became suspicious. I never entered his study except to bring him something. He turned up his nose, pretending to sniff the air. This was his way of asking what I wanted.

"We'll be having dinner an hour earlier than usual," I said with a vague laugh, "because we're going to leave at six and need time to get ready." Hoping this would satisfy him, I quickly judged the length and height I'd need. A sake box wouldn't be wide enough—even one for two bottles. He'd be able to fit, but there'd be no room to spare. Then it came to me—what about that honey box? Both my husband and mother-in-law love Chinese milk vetch honey. As it's much cheaper if you buy a nine-pound bottle, my mother-in-law ordered one directly from a honey supplier out in the country somewhere, but the bottle it came in was so big and heavy not even

I could pick it up, and so I ended up dragging it around. Did we still have the box? It might be with the burnable trash. I went to look and was relieved to find it there. There were vegetable scraps stuck to it, and I'd started to fold it so it would burn more quickly. I hadn't in the end, though; the cardboard was so thick I'd gone to get a knife to cut it down, then got distracted and forgot about it. If I wiped off the outside and straightened it out, it would do just fine. It was plenty wide. The only problem was that it wasn't quite tall enough. If my husband sat down inside it, the top of his head would peek out. His hat, maybe. My husband liked hats. He had a fine, soft felt hat; a hunting cap; a beret; a baseball cap; a summer hat with a wide brim; and a wool knit cap with a pompom. I could hardly imagine him bareheaded. He even wore a night cap to bed. Not that he was bald, but he was apparently a little self-conscious about how flat the top of his head was. Besides, hats suited him. Most of his were actually for children, to wear when they got dressed up to go to a shrine for the Seven-Five-Three Festival. Even so, they were so big on him they covered half his face. His glasses, low down on his nose, sat right below the hat, so it was hard to really see his face. But I could always tell how he was feeling from his subtle movements and gestures. While he was in the box, a rather small hat would be best. His hunting cap, or the beret, maybe. I didn't care for the beret—it looked too cartoonish. I wanted him to wear his English checkered hunting cap, but if given the choice, he'd probably take the beret. He didn't like the hunting cap. I'd also have to get a smaller box for him to sit on, so he could peek out of the big box during the opera.

    I was thinking about all these things during lunch and while washing the dishes afterward, so I didn't even remember eating. I marched mechanically out into the garden to bring in the laundry. My mother-in-law stayed shut up in her room. She usually came out to help, since some of the clean clothes were hers, and she could see the laundry poles from her window. She hadn't said a word at lunch. Her lower lip was pressed into a straight line, moving to one side or quivering only when she ate. She scowled over at me now and then, or intentionally turned away from my husband as she sipped the sauce she'd dipped her noodles in. She must have been in a bad mood. "You needn't fix dinner for me," she'd said after lunch. "I'll eat at the usual time. I don't have to hurry. And don't bother making anything for me, either. I'll make do on my own." After she'd left, I said to my husband, "Maybe it would have been better to buy Mother a ticket, too." He glanced over at me and wiggled an ear. My mother-in-law wasn't interested in classical music. Perhaps it would be better to say she hated it. Her taste in TV programs was completely different from ours, too, so she always watched in her own room.

I'd carry the box wrapped in a furoshiki, I thought as I carelessly folded up the laundry. Did we have a furoshiki that would be big enough? The only one I could think of was green with a clear, white scrollwork pattern. There was an old, russet-brown one as well. It was torn in places, with patches clumsily sewn on. I'd never seen my mother-in-law with a needle and thread, so someone else must have patched it. That furoshiki had been in the family for generations. So had several other things in this house. An old brass figurine that might have been a horse, a cow, or a deer. My mother-in-law called it *Fushizō*. Then there was a round foot warmer, and a mallet for pounding straw she called *Kinuta* that looked like the magic one in the old stories that you strike to get whatever you want. I'd screamed once when I opened a box of what looked like dozens of dead baby mice. They were actually tiny foxes, badgers, rabbits, turtles, sparrows, and other animals made of faded crepe, with cotton coming out of the seams, wrinkled and bunched up together so that they looked like a pile of dead mice. "Passed down from our ancestors," my mother-in-law had said, as though they were nothing special. I never saw her mending them, either.

I'd brought the furoshiki with the scrollwork pattern with me, so the cloth was still new, but it would stand out too much.

The brown one wouldn't attract so much attention. I decided not to think about whether the color would clash with my pale-blue summer coat.

Since we'd be eating by ourselves, dinner didn't have to start at five. We could have it at four-thirty, or even four o'clock for that matter. Any time would be fine. We had lots of practicing to do before we went out tonight. For starters, I wasn't sure if the box I'd chosen was really the right size. As soon as I'd finished putting the clean laundry away, I brought the box with my husband's seat inside, plus the furoshiki, to my husband's study.

"We can have dinner anytime," I said. "There's so much we have to do before we leave."

"Right," he said, just as I'd thought he would. When I put the box in a corner, he turned around, his nose twitching, and stared at it. This was not a good sign. He didn't like it. But what did he expect me to do? I slipped out to the kitchen to start dinner. While I was slicing tomatoes, I heard a great thud from the living room. Along with what sounded like a moan. I ran to the living room and saw that the box had fallen over. My husband had gotten in, then when he'd tried to get out it had fallen over, and the flaps of the lid that I had folded back had flopped back down again. High-pitched cries came from inside. I opened the lid, and my husband crawled out. His fine hair was a mess, standing on end.

"How was it?" I asked. "Too cramped? I don't think we have any others we can use."

"Bue," he said. This wasn't an expression of dissatisfaction, though—it was more like, "Good grief." After getting back into position in the box with his hat on his head—the beret, just as I'd thought—he asked, "Think you'll be able to carry it? Pretty heavy, isn't it?" He, too, realized that there was no other way.

"I'll be fine," I replied, looking out the window. It looked like it would start raining any minute, which worried me. It wouldn't be easy, carrying this big box with my umbrella up, and my handbag besides, but I wasn't going to let that keep me from seeing *The Magic Flute*. I was determined not to give up this chance for happiness. My husband would probably be hearing the opera live for the first time in his life. "I'll be fine," I said once more, and went back to the kitchen.

We finished dinner so quickly it was almost scary. We only ate about five bites each. Afterward, we practiced with the box. It was heavy. But I'd only have to walk about 55 yards or so to the bus stop, and after we got off at Taka-machi, another 200 yards to the concert hall. There's a slope to climb from the bus stop, I was thinking, when I heard my husband say, "Call for a taxi." It was hard to hear him from inside the box. His voice is normally very soft. He only lets out loud, high-pitched cries in moments of desperation.

There was a clump of fish mint growing under the snowbell tree in the garden. The white flowers stood out against the dark green of the leaves. From far away, the plants just looked green, but when you got up close, you saw a deep purple like blood in the leaves and stems. My mother-in-law left the fish mint alone when she weeded the garden, so I followed suit.

"Lizard tail plants are so refreshing to look at," she'd once said. I'd thought she must be talking about the fish mint, but just to be sure, I'd asked her. "Is that what you call them?" she'd mused. "Well, they're probably pretty much the same thing." So now I also call them "lizard tails," too. Though I've always known about fish mint, lizard tails are new to me, but I figure they must look very much alike.

The opera was absolutely wonderful. My husband tapped his foot to the rhythm from inside the box, quietly humming along with "Papageno, Papagena," and frequently commenting on how weak the string section was. This was intended as praise, rather than criticism. I could tell because he often said that when he was enthusiastic about a CD he was listening to.

He seemed to find going out as interesting as the opera itself. After that first outing, I cut a hole in the box so he could see out, and bought a new furoshiki, thin enough for him to see through. There was a vacant lot on the corner that we had to cut through to get to the main road no matter where we were going. It was a grassy area, about 790 square yards, marked off by rope stretched among the four poles at the corners, so I had to step over the ropes to cross it. It was also a popular toilet for the neighborhood cats and dogs. At meetings of the Neighborhood Association, people often complained about what a mess it was, and how no one bothered to clean it up, but to my husband, it was a whole new world, where he saw azaleas, and cattails, and dayflowers swaying in the breeze, and where he could watch grasshoppers and frogs jump, right in front of him. "Yah!" he'd call from inside the box, or "Oh!" When he called my attention to snails or praying mantises with a high-pitched cry, I had to stop right there.

"I won't be long," I'd say when I was getting ready to go out, and he'd let out a sharp sigh that sounded something like "Shue." It seemed to come out naturally. Though I knew it meant "I want to go, too," I couldn't take him on days when I had lots to buy, so I'd pretend I hadn't noticed and leave by myself. He never actually came out and announced that he was going too. I wouldn't have minded taking him for a walk or to the park, but the park was pretty far away. And we couldn't go for walks every day. Even on my bicycle it was nearly ten minutes to the Taisei Supermarket, which was cheap and had the best selection, so I couldn't very well take the box. There wouldn't be enough room for the shopping bags, and besides, the box would sway back and forth on the bike. I was awfully busy that year. The rainy season dragged on and on, so whenever the sun came out, I was busy doing the laundry or rushing to the grocery store. And there was another reason why I had so much to do. Ever since that opera, my mother-in-law had completely stopped doing the household chores she'd done before. Previously, she'd helped me with the laundry and the cooking and had always taken charge of getting the bath ready. She'd swept the area around the entrance way, and cleaned the toilet, too. Now she didn't do any of that and seemed to be avoiding me. She'd always gone out twice a week, to her lessons in Noh chanting and folk songs, but now she left the house practically every day. I had no idea where she went. Sometimes she'd buy herself some food to eat alone in her room. When I went to tell her dinner was ready, she'd say, "I've already had mine, so I don't want anything," and wouldn't come out, or even open the door. There were days when she even neglected to cut out newspaper clippings for my husband. Only when he reminded her did she finally start looking through the paper.

It looked as if it might start pouring any time that day, so I was planning to ignore my husband's demands and ride my bike to the Taisei Supermarket. As there were more cash registers there, I'd be able to pay and leave quickly. Five-packs of tissue boxes were on sale, and I was planning to buy a bag of rice as well, which meant the basket in front and the carrier in back would both be full. In response to my husband's "Shue," I told him, "I have lots to buy today, so I'll be riding my bicycle." Normally, that would have been enough to quiet him, but today, he insisted on going. I realized then that he hadn't been outside for a whole week.

"I understand," I said, "but please wait just one more day. I promise we'll go out tomorrow."

"No. Today," was his reply. I looked at him, stunned. He had a grim, positively nasty look on his face, his forehead creased with vertical wrinkles. I changed plans, opting for the neighborhood supermarket. With him along, all I'd be able to buy was long green onions, sesame seeds, and kitchen detergent. The entrance to that supermarket was crowded with trays of vegetables on sale, with stray, torn-off leaves, sheets of newspaper and wrapping paper, and cardboard boxes scattered around. A stream of water from the fish shop next door kept it wet and dark even when it wasn't raining. I bought ginger and garlic, even though we still had some. My husband didn't like smelly things like that. I put them in a plastic shopping bag that hung down next to his box. A supermarket isn't a very interesting place, so why come? I thought. All he could see were stacks of cans, bottles of vegetable oil, bags of snacks, and vegetables rushing by. And on the way home, he'd be choking on the smell of ginger and garlic. I wanted him to see things that way.

I got through the checkout line and was coming out the narrow entrance when someone ran straight into me. Though I swerved to avoid him, it was too late, and I ended up slipping, falling off the bike. My plastic shopping bags went flying. Flustered, the young man who'd run into me apologized and helped me pick the things up. The box had fallen over, so I stood it up and looked inside. Being heavy, it had fallen at my feet, so I thought there wouldn't be much damage. But my husband was limp, lying on the bottom with his legs in the air. I asked him if he was all right and got no answer. When I picked up the box, he slipped right through the bottom. Had the bottom fallen out when the man ran into me? He was still standing there, so I turned to him and said, "Something terrible has happened. Please call an ambulance."

At the hospital, they laid my husband on a gurney. They were pretty quick about that, but then things seemed to stop there. No one came to treat him. Though completely unconscious, he was having spasms. Finally, a doctor and nurse came to look at him. The doctor lifted his shirt and felt his stomach, then pulled back his eyelids. "He looks like an old man, but he's actually quite young," the doctor said to the nurse, who replied, "Yes, he's much younger than he looks." Why were they talking about his age? Why didn't they hurry up and do something for him, I thought, getting more and more irritated. About half an hour later, they wheeled him into a back room and told me to wait in the corridor outside. Looking out the small window, I saw that it was raining. The corridor was long, and dimly lit, and it seemed as if my husband would never come out. I discovered a public telephone tucked away in a corner. I'd have to phone my mother-in-law. She'd been out when we left, but she was probably back by now.

"It was all my fault," I said. "I fell down in front of the supermarket—the one near us... That's right, after I was through the checkout line, and was starting for home. We're at the hospital now, but he's still unconscious." I started to cry and couldn't say any more.

"You shouldn't have taken him outside," she said. "I knew something like this would happen." She didn't sound surprised, or particularly angry, either. "He isn't dead, is he? Where did he hurt himself?"

"I don't know. He isn't bleeding, but I think he may have hit his head."

"He'll be fine then," she said. "This happens all the time. I've just started making fig jam, so I can't get away just now," she went on, "besides, there are preparations I have to make, but I'll be along as soon as I can." Then she hung up.

There was nothing to do but wait. One hour seemed like ten. Two more emergency patients were brought in while I was waiting, and a gust of damp, cold air came in with them. There was a family waiting on the bench next to me. A couple in their thirties, with a baby. They didn't talk at all, so I had no idea who they were waiting for. Did they have an older child who was sick, or had one of their parents who lived with them suddenly taken ill? Now and then I heard a baby crying beyond the heavy door. Each time, the couple stared in that direction. The baby the wife was holding was tiny, probably under six months. Did they have one more? Twins, perhaps?

I felt off balance. My husband seemed about to die any minute, yet my mother-in-law talked as if there was nothing to worry about. Irritation and tears collected in my eyes, then sort of vaguely melted away and things went back to normal. I felt my neck sinking into my torso.

Suddenly, my mother-in-law was standing in front of me.

"Relax, everything's going to be fine," she said cheerfully, placing the bags she was carrying on the bench with a thud. "Where's the stuff you bought at the supermarket? You did the shopping, didn't you?"

My mouth must have fallen open. I'd forgotten all about that; I'd probably gotten into the ambulance with just my handbag.

"Well, don't worry about it. Where is he? I have to give him his milk before it gets cold. He's crying, isn't he? He always does."

My mother-in-law opened the heavy door to the back room and marched right in. My husband was still lying on the gurney he'd been brought in on. No one else was around. The doctors and nurses must have all been in the operating room farther back; I heard footsteps back and forth, and voices. "Unya, unya," my husband cried, so loudly it surprised me. This was the voice I'd heard while I was waiting on the bench. "There, there," my mother-in-law said as she took a baby bottle out of her furoshiki and brought it to his lips. As he sucked on the nipple, he looked at me out of the corner of his eye. That, at least, was normal. He'd always tended to look at me sideways rather than head on.

"You're all right, I'm so relieved," I said, sinking down to a crouch, clinging to my husband. "I was afraid you might die." As my tension eased, the tears came gushing out. "I'm so sorry. We'll go for a walk every day from now on. I'll do whatever you say, so please forgive me." I was weeping the whole time. My husband let go of the nipple and said, "Bue." I couldn't tell whether or not he meant that as a reply.

"You listen here," my mother-in-law scolded, "you should never have taken him outside in the first place." She took out a swaddling blanket, wrapped my husband in it, and picked him up. "He won't understand anything you say for a while now. This is chronic with him—he gets this way now and then. I'm going to take him home now, but I'll let you out on the way so you can buy formula and diapers. We'll need lots of them."

She was energized. "We're going to be really busy from now on," she said as we walked to the taxi stand in front of the hospital. She was small and very thin, though, carrying a baby who was much too big for her, so she didn't exactly sweep briskly along. The hem of the blanket dragged on the ground as she staggered under his weight.

From then on, my husband slept in my mother-in-law's room. There were night feedings, she said, and he cried several times during the night. She changed his diapers and gave him his bath. When I protested, "I'll do it—he's my husband," she snorted with laughter.

"He needs his mother. You're totally useless. Just tend to the housework, as you've always done."

Though it seemed that my husband was merely sleeping in a different room, the change went much deeper. Before, we had talked to each other, and occasionally argued. His subtle movements had told me everything. And he'd understood me completely, too. I'd been happy, wrapped in the existence of my tiny husband. But where was he now? Not here. I wanted him back, but when I searched for even a fragment of his former self, I found only a baby crying "Unya, unya." When he wasn't crying, he gave me sidelong looks, showing the whites of his eyes, staring at me as if I were some strange creature. The color returned to my mother-in-law's cheeks, making her look much younger. I fixed soft baby food, washed diapers, boiled water. At night I heard lullabies from my mother-in-law's room. Buddhist hymns, perhaps. Or maybe she was talking to herself, rhythmically. As my husband spent the whole day in her room, I only caught glimpses of him when I had an excuse to go in there.

Toward the end of summer, I couldn't stand it anymore. "What will become of him?" I asked my mother-in-law, "Is he going to stay this way?" He needed to get some sun now and then, so she was letting him play on the veranda outside the living room. The veins in the fish mint plants had turned brown, and the wind whipped up the porcelain berry vines clinging to the torn net over the bamboo fence. Due to a typhoon that had just missed us, the wind was strong that day. "How long will it take for him to get over this?" I asked. "Do these spells happen often?"

"Let's see…" she replied. "This is the third or fourth time, I guess. It usually passes eventually, but how long is hard to tell—could be a week, or six months. It may take years. This time it seems kind of serious. Maybe we should go back to

Bakinu. He might get better faster there. If the head of the Wiod Clan examines him, he may know what to do."

"Let's go then. Let's leave tomorrow. I want to do everything I can for him."

My mother-in-law gave me a funny look. The wrinkles around her nose looked just like my husband's.

"You can't come. After all, you're just a servant."

"I am not. I'm not the maid—I'm his wife."

"Someone as big as you are, his wife? Makes me laugh—me and everybody else, too. Where did you get that idea? If they hear about this in Bakinu, there'll be hell to pay. Don't tell me you thought you were married to him all this time. Incredible."

"Ah, uh, well, I..." I was much too shocked to say anything. We *were* husband and wife—I knew it. Was she joking? *You know I'm your wife*, I said silently to my husband. *Please tell her. Say something.*

My mouth opened, then closed, then opened again. I felt something pulling at my knees. The baby had crawled over to me and was clutching my skirt in his hand. When my mother-in-law saw that, she took hold of his legs and tried to pull him back toward her, but he wouldn't let go. Moaning, he clung to my skirt with all his strength. His drool was seeping into my knees. "Bue, bue," he said. I realized that this meant "Wait a little longer," and suddenly, I felt perfectly calm.

"I don't need to go to Bakinu," I said. "Because it won't be long now. Until then, I'll take care of him. I'll cure him. You can think of me as a servant or whatever you want. My husband doesn't agree."

He was still clinging to my knees. My mother-in-law stared vaguely out into the garden. "You should weed the place once in a while," she said. "After the lizard tails wilt, pick them and steep them for tea. They say lizard tail tea makes a good sedative."

My mother-in-law was sitting flat on her bottom. I peered into her face and saw that her features seemed to have gathered toward the middle, and that the tip of her nose was dark. The gray hair that grew in clumps behind her ears hung down to her chin. The two long curved front teeth that protruded from her half-open mouth were just like my husband's.

つけ髭

Taruho Inagaki

The False Mustache

Translated by Jeffrey Angles

The False Mustache

EVEN THOUGH THE BOY WAS ALREADY IN MIDDLE SCHOOL, he was still terrified to strike a match, so much so, in fact, that he was never quite sure whether he'd succeed in lighting it or accidentally throw the matchstick from his fingers. Likewise, whenever he saw two samurai clash and draw their swords in movies, he couldn't even raise his head to look at the screen. And yet, the boy was in seventh heaven whenever a band of men, clustered in tight formation or mounted on horses, started firing rifles and pistols, letting out phantasmal puffs of white smoke. Such things recalled something he'd once seen in a movie somewhere.

The scene featured a group of soldiers next to a bunch of tents set up in the flatlands at the foot of some mountains. Surrounding the soldiers was a group of mounted Indians on the attack. The soldiers had formed a large circle around the tents to try to fight off the Indians, who were concentrating all their firepower on them as they spurred their horses on, racing around them. The soldiers fell one after another. The Stars and Stripes peeked through the clouds of white smoke, flapping in the air as if trying to alert everyone to the disaster that was unfolding. The flag fluttering back and forth was so beautiful that the boy hardly knew how to put it into words, and even now, much later, he could easily summon up the vision of it. But the scene that really captured the boy's heart was the short one that followed.

The attack was over. The flag had been wrenched from the flagpole, and the tents had been ripped down and trampled—everything was in complete disarray. Meanwhile, the moon was shining overhead as if nothing were the matter—the film had been colored to give it a bluish tinge—but there in the flatlands between the hills, in the midst of all the confusion, which was so terrible that at first he couldn't quite understand what he was seeing, there were heaps and heaps of corpses of nude soldiers—yes, that's right—without even a single stitch of clothing. When he realized what he was seeing, the boy stared at the screen with eyes wide open in surprise. Was it really okay to film a scene like that? He did his best to take in the entire pile of soft, white shapes as quickly as possible, while trying to figure out which body part belonged to which body. What had happened to that hand? Why was that leg over there? How were those parts between the trunks of the bodies connected? The naked corpses were piled together in utter confusion, with no rhyme or reason at all. The boy felt anxious as he rushed to take it in. The scene that appeared momentarily on the screen was so confused that he couldn't make heads or tails of it at first. But a few seconds later, he finally understood—the white lump on the left edge of the vivid mountain of flesh was actually a body whose head was hidden, stuck among the layers of folded limbs belonging to the other soldiers; only two-thirds of the upside-down body was exposed. The way the body bent made it look like the soldier was taking a deep, uncomfortable bow; however, the simple fact that this appeared under the pale moonlight up on the silver screen gave it a suggestive, sensual beauty. Even after the film moved on to show a rescue party departing, even after the film ended and the lights went up in the theater, and in fact, even as the boy was on his way home, he found himself unable to think about anything but the curve of that body.

Although he vividly remembered the scene, he didn't think he'd be able to reenact it at home in private, like he had done with certain scenes after seeing other movies—a detective tied to the railway tracks, a young girl trapped in a box, or a pilot crushed underneath his smashed airplane... Those other scenes had also made his heart race, but this time, merely imagining tonight's scene and adopting the deep, bowing posture of the soldier wouldn't be enough to satisfy him. It wouldn't be enough unless he tried to replicate the feel of a cold, moonlit night at the foot of the mountains by taking off half of his clothes and exposing his skin. Still, he didn't think he could go all the way. What would happen if someone walked in on him while he was acting so strangely? — Before long, however, he realized that he could strip completely naked in bed, especially after the lights had gone out. He tried it that very night, but still it wasn't enough to satisfy him. Then a few nights later, he noticed a figure pressed against the railing of the spiral staircase leading up to his room on the second floor.

Earlier that evening, he had crawled out of his futon and had tried two or three times on the cold tatami mats to imitate the soldier who had died deep in the mountains, bathed in moonlight. — Later, in the first-floor hallway, the boy pricked up his ears, listening for any sign of his family. The coast was clear. Next, he turned his attention toward the dark, camphor-scented room across the way. Of course, no one was there either. The only thing he saw was the faint, melancholy sparkle of the nickel and glass objects in the room catching the last light of twilight trickling through the window frame. In the hallway, someone had switched on a nightlight, and directly across from it were a pair of frosted-glass, paneled doors that opened to either side. To reach these doors, someone would have to first open another door near the front entrance. If someone was coming, he would hear and have a few seconds to cover himself up. Even so, there was no way he'd take off all his clothes right there. He rolled up the bottom of his kimono so that his body was exposed from the hips down, and he stuffed the underwear he had removed into his pocket. — Perhaps this way, he could experience at least half of the sensation of the defeated soldier who had been stripped naked and thrown aside after his defeat, deep in the lonely wilderness of the barren mountains. He kneeled on the floor, folded his hands behind his back, leaned forward, and stuck his bottom out. He turned his head to the side, and with his mind resolutely made up, he fell forward so that his shoulders pressed against the floor in front of him—he imagined he'd been discarded by feather-adorned Indians after they had used him repeatedly as their toy. The floor was linoleum; he pressed his body against it so that he could feel as much of its hard coldness as possible... He placed his cheek flat against the hallway floor. Wondering how he looked, he tried to check himself out in the large mirror on the wall, but he was so low to the floor he couldn't see himself. He lifted his face and checked to see if he could make the line of white skin from his lower back to his thighs resemble the curve of the fallen soldier. With effort, perhaps—he had to hold his lower body still, since the position immediately became extremely uncomfortable. Once he had ascertained that he had succeeded in forming the right kind of curve, he once again pressed his cheek against the linoleum to imitate the soldier's form. In the process, he turned his head to the side and glanced upward. The base of the spiral staircase that connected the multiple floors of the house was right by his feet, and as he glanced up, he saw a young man staring down at him.

Surprised, the boy found himself momentarily unable to move; then, as he jumped to his feet, he felt his face flush bright red. — The young man he had seen was a smart, college-aged student who had come from the same province as the boy's father, and had been living with the boy's family while going to medical school. The young man would have graduated in the spring of that year, but according to a shocking story that the boy had heard from the nurse who worked in his father's pharmacy, which was attached to the home, something bad had happened. The young man had been visiting someone's house and had been cavorting with the wife when her husband suddenly came home and found them together. It caused a huge fuss, and the husband threatened to sue the young man. The story would have been in the papers before long if the boy's father had not finally stepped in to keep a lid on the whole affair. The young man was temporarily suspended, but he was trying to get back in the school's good graces by spending most of his time at the boy's house studying under close observation. Until about two years ago, the young man had sometimes taken the boy to play in the park or to do other things, but the boy had still been young at the time, and there had been many things the boy still hadn't understood. The boy's impressions of the young man were not all that remarkable—he was a young man of few words, pretty, and his fingernails were always well manicured, but beyond that, the boy didn't think about him much. He didn't particularly like him, but he didn't dislike him either. Still, when their eyes met, the boy would sometimes do unusual things like follow the young man back to his room on the second floor. The young man tended to hole himself up awkwardly in his room, and sometimes the boy would join him. There, the boy would gaze at rare and unusual fragments of things through the young man's microscope, and the young man would give him small little bottles of cobalt blue and brown glass with stoppered lids. However, that was all.

The young man seemed to be walking down the stairs toward him. He had been taking in the boy's embarrassing behavior, which the boy now realized would be impossible to explain. He was so ashamed he wanted to burst into tears. He ought to run away as fast as he could. But even running away at the first possible opportunity wouldn't solve anything; it would just lead to more problems. As the boy got to his feet, he looked up once again at the young man, who seemed to be smiling slightly now. That helped break the ice. With a smile creeping onto his face, the boy started climbing the stairs. The movements came of their own accord, as if he wasn't aware of what he was doing. But, what else could he have done? The boy passed the young man on the stairs and, reaching the top, quietly walked through the door into his room.

The lamp with the blue umbrella shade on the mahogany desk was still on, and it cast a circle of light on the thick, German book open underneath. The boy walked up to the desk, sat down, and began staring at the book's colorful red and blue anatomical drawings as if trying to lose himself in them. He still felt ill at ease. He had been feeling terribly awkward since noticing the young man's presence, and he still wasn't entirely sure what to do. Old memories bubbled up from the depths of his mind, only to be replaced by others right away. The young man lingered on the staircase in apparent surprise, but after a few moments, he walked back into his room where the boy was waiting and sat down beside him. Then, he placed an unpleasantly soft hand on the boy's shoulder.

"Does this interest you?"

"What...this?" The boy's voice sounded rather hoarse.

"Tell me. What's going on?"

As he spoke, the young man turned and pulled the boy into an embrace. Then, as if none of this were out of the ordinary at all, he pressed his cheek against the boy's, before turning to take in his entire countenance. Holding the boy's face between his two hands, the young man turned the boy toward him and kissed him on the lips. The boy was motionless, unable to do a thing. Just then, he heard the nurse calling out from the foot of the staircase. The young man called back animatedly, "I hear you... Coming..." but before walking down the stairs, he swiftly wiped the boy's lips with the sleeve of his *Kurume-kasuri* kimono. After the young man left, the boy was left all alone on the second floor. He felt relieved, as if he'd made his way through some checkpoint, but gazing into the small round mirror sitting on top of the desk, he noticed that both of his eyelids now had a deep, second fold running horizontally across them. He tried blinking and rubbing his eyelids with his fingers, but they didn't return to normal. A new, different type of worry began to well up inside of him. Without a sound, he crept down the stairs from the second floor, entered his older sister's room, pulled a brush out of her vanity, and began tapping his cheeks with it to coat them with white powder.

One night about a week later, the boy received an order from the young man as he brushed by him—there was a Boy Scout uniform hanging on the wall, and the young man ordered him to change into it. The order seemed to him to come out of the blue, as if from a stranger passing him on a staircase or in a bend in the hallway, and yet the boy didn't feel he had any choice but to obey. — That first night, after embracing the boy from behind, the young man had placed the boy briefly on his lap. The next day, he'd sat the boy on his lap facing him, and the day after that, they'd done the same thing again, then rolled around on the tatami floor together. The boy had stuck out his lips as though about to smile. It was clear that he was enjoying their games together. That's why he felt he had little choice but to obey when the young man ordered him to change into the uniform.

That evening brought more games. After the two sat down together, the young man commented that he'd seen the boy make a strange face earlier when, hearing some footsteps upstairs, he'd looked out to see the young man's friend from school coming down the stairs. Then there was the time the young man had picked up the boy in both arms and carried him down to the ground floor. The boy was nervous and excited, but then, just as he had feared, the door that led into the living quarters of the house from the boy's father's pharmacy next door swung open to reveal the nurse's pale face.

"My goodness, I thought everyone was out. What're you two up to?"

The young man, however, didn't lose his cool. He just said, "This would look bad if he was a girl!" With those words hanging in the air, the young man continued heavily down to the bottom of the stairs, still holding the boy in his arms as if nothing was the matter. He didn't put him down until they reached the sink. It was a perfect spot. Although the light was on, the place where the young man's hand was touching him was bathed in shadow so there's no way the nurse would have noticed.

Once when the boy came home from school, he went upstairs and took off his clothes as if it were summer. The young man had earlier suggested wrestling, and so the boy got himself all ready, but so much time passed that the boy began to doubt the young man would even come to see him on the second floor that day. Their secret games continued until one evening about a week later when everyone was out of the house. The boy was wearing the Boy Scout uniform again, just like the young man liked, when the young man brought up the awkwardness that had transpired that first night. The boy had almost forgotten about it.

—— Someone looking down from the top of the stairs shouldn't have been able to figure out what the boy's strange behavior meant. That's why the boy was so astonished when the young man said, "As soon as you get to that spot on the second floor, fall over like you've been shot." However, before the boy knew it, the young man took him in his arms, carried him to the precise location, and placed him lying face down. He had the boy bend both of his knees so that he took on the same posture as that first night when the young man had seen him from the stairs. He immediately turned off the tabletop lamp and switched on the overhead light so that the boy was bathed in bluish shade. Dim light washed over the room like in the nighttime scene from the movie. The young man went to the front door and brought back a pair of shoes from the shoe cabinet. He put them on the boy's feet and carefully tied the laces. The young man was clad in a sky-blue uniform with red piping, like a military uniform from some foreign country. On his feet were a pair of red leather boots that were so shiny they practically twinkled. He was also wearing a military helmet. It was the real thing—on the top was a short, little spear. The young man told the boy that a friend had recently given it to him, a present from Germany. Later that evening, when the nurse came in late, opened the front door, and found the young man wearing the demonic-looking thing on his head, she was so taken aback by the odd vision that she slammed the door shut with a *wham!* After that, the helmet became one of their favorite toys. In addition to the helmet and the uniform, the young man had a saber, making his outfit complete. The boy had no idea when or why the young man had acquired all those things, but when the young man stood there in the pale light, the outfit looked so good on him that the boy began to believe the young man really was a foreign military officer. Until then, when confronted with these unusual situations, the boy had been full of anxiety, thinking perhaps they should stop fooling around, but now that they had the costumes, whenever they started playing one of their strange games, the boy also began to feel like someone else entirely, and curiosity bubbled up within him. Where would these games lead? He wanted to see them through to the very end.

"A virtuous young soldier has fallen. He is lying on an embankment on the front lines in northern France, as the light of the moon shines down. Overhead, searchlights swing back and forth, forming shifting stripes of light in the sky, white with smoke from all the exploding shells. We'll have to use fireworks to produce that effect. I'll look into it…"

The helmeted officer delivered this prologue like he was narrating the action of a film. Although he had already blindfolded the boy with a handkerchief, he removed the boy's hat, then readjusted it on his head with the chin straps dangling loose so it looked like the hat was about to slide off. He tugged on the boy's neckerchief, adjusted the angles of the boy's shoes, spread the boy's thighs so that they opened wider, then lifted the boy's lower back so that his bottom stuck out a little more…

The False Mustache

The young man adjusted the boy, manhandling him in all sorts of ways as if giving him a rough physical exam. Then, from what the boy could tell from beneath his blindfold, the young man stepped back to admire his handiwork. He gazed at the boy for what felt like quite a long time. After a while, the boy heard the rattling of the saber and the squeak of the young man's boots. They were coming from outside the room, probably partway up the staircase. Then, slowly, the young man began creeping stealthily back toward him. The boy could hear his own heart pounding hard in his chest as he felt the hard toe of a boot press firmly against his shoulder. The young man pushed him as if kicking him, and the fallen soldier's slender body rolled onto its side. A little more, and the boy found himself facing upward. The young man's knees pressed between the boy's thighs, covered in nothing but shorts, and as he did so, the boy sensed the officer's aroma enveloping him—a combination of leather and wool. Right then, the officer took one of the boy's arms and placed it over his shoulder. As the officer lifted him in his arms, the boy felt like a fourteen-year-old bride. He trembled slightly but remained limp as if he really were an unconscious young soldier. He felt the blue, electric moon on his eyelids, and he closed his eyes all the tighter. The enemy officer had approached him from behind, by his feet, drawing in close as if wanting to take in the fallen soldier's scent, and when the fallen soldier felt the officer kiss him on the lips, he couldn't help wondering for a moment if the bushy thing he felt brushing against him hadn't been there from the very start.

箱の夫

Hot Day

Takako Takahashi

Translated by Brian Bergstrom

Hot Day

I SHOULD HAVE BROUGHT A PARASOL, THOUGHT THE WOMAN. But her body was so hot that the idea of voicing the thought aloud seemed too much trouble. The heat rose up within her, its sound a dull roar lodged in her throat. *I should have brought a parasol.* How many times had she had the thought today? But a parasol would only help with the heat outside, she realized. It would do nothing for the heat within.

"It's still pretty far."

The man raised an arm to point vaguely in front of them.

"But we're going?"

The woman spoke. Hot, wet air clung to her mouth.

It was the man who'd suggested walking to the end of the pier. Tall concrete breakwaters fanned out on both sides of the wharf, the one to the left following the water's edge before extending into the sea to become a pier. They were at the very tip of a peninsula. Its midsection was too rocky to be developed properly, so the tip was inaccessible even by bus. The only way in or out was by sea.

"It really is so hot here."

The man scraped the soles of his leather shoes against the ground as he walked. He spoke as if only just remembering the heat.

"Is there anything out there?"

The woman gazed ahead, seeing a long, white concrete line shimmering in the sun and nothing else.

"What else are we going to do before the next boat comes in?"

His words sounded casual, but there was nothing casual about how he strode on ahead.

"I still can't believe they didn't have a room."

The woman looked out at the surface of the sea, flat as a sheet of stainless steel. The wind had stopped completely. But could there really be no wind at all by the sea? Wasn't there always at least a little salt-scented breeze riffling the air, even as the midsummer sun beat down? But everything around her, the air included, was absolutely still, as if holding its breath in anticipation. Of what? A sudden downpour? An even greater heat, enough to burn the very thoughts from her head?

"Did it ever occur to you that they might not have a room for us?"

The woman didn't mean this as a reproach.

The man and the woman had decided to spend this mid-August Sunday afternoon here, at the tip of this peninsula, together. Separated from the city by the span of the sea, they were safe from the eyes of others. They knew there were only two small inns here. It was nothing more than an old, run-down fishing port without even a proper swimming area, so you would think no one would be trying to stay here outside the occasional fisherman. Their plan was to spend five hours together in a room in an otherwise vacant, off-season inn. The man had to be home that night. But when they arrived, both inns were inexplicably full.

"No vacancy?" asked the woman, flustered, at the first inn's entrance.

"All rooms have been reserved already. So, no, I'm afraid there is no vacancy at the moment, as you can see."

The innkeeper gestured at the array of shoes and straw sandals lined up at the entrance.

"Who are all these people?"

The woman's voice rose shrilly, prompting the man to tug at the hem of her blouse from behind.

"No vacancy? Really?" asked the woman at the second inn, overcome with shock.

"I'm afraid there's nothing I can do," said the second innkeeper, as if anticipating her reaction.

Hot Day

A silk gauze noren divided the entrance from the next room, long enough to reach from the lintel to the floor. It hung straight down, completely motionless. It was so insubstantial that she could see the small Buddhist altar set up in the next room; it presided over a large table covered with offerings of sweet potatoes, eggplant, and tomatoes, along with bouquets of flowers and paper lanterns with scenes painted on them. The special abundance of Obon season somehow suited the stifling heat.

"There isn't a room where we could stay for just a little while?"
The woman insisted.
"I'm very sorry."
The innkeeper bowed his head again and again in apology.
"Could we wait here until one frees up?"
"Everyone has reserved their rooms for the night as well."

Even then, the woman showed no signs of budging from the inn's entrance, prompting the man to tug at the back of her blouse once more. They returned to the wharf. The next boat back to the city was due to arrive at half past three. It was now noon. Contemplating spending the next three and a half hours unable to be alone with the man, the woman let out a despairing sigh. It was just before Obon, so people returning home for the holiday may have decided to rent out rooms in an inn instead of trying to fit everyone into their cramped homes in the city, and it was a Sunday besides, so some others may have come to fish as well. This was the man's explanation. In any case, he went on, being surrounded by occupied rooms on all sides wouldn't have been that fun either. The woman contemplated spending all the time she'd set aside for their rendezvous unable to do anything else on this isolated tip of the peninsula but sizzle beneath the burning sun.

"You're going to burn," said the man, his soles still scuffing the concrete as he walked.

"I should have brought a parasol," said the woman, finally giving voice to the thought she'd been having all day, though it seemed hardly any different to say it than to think it.

"Here, wear this."

The man took off his wide-brimmed hat and handed it to the woman.

The woman took it, sneaking a glance at the man as she did. Without his hat, his thinning hairline stood out on his forehead. The man returned her glance. The woman felt it hit her body, a straight line of pure greed as if he were an animal laying eyes on its next meal. Then he looked away, resuming his steady march toward the pier.

The woman put the man's hat on her head. The familiar smell of hair oil pricked her nose. And deep within it, the heavy smell of his sweat.

"What is it?"

The man stopped and turned back to the woman, who'd remained fixed to the spot as he'd walked on.

"Oh—nothing. It's nothing."

The woman had been lost in the man's smell, but she snapped back to herself and caught up.

"I don't mind getting a bit tan, but your skin is so delicate."

The man's voice seemed strangely sticky, clinging to her like the smell from his hat.

"It gets red so fast…"

The woman thought about her skin, about how easily it became marked by the sun, or even by the slightest friction. Fishnet stockings would leave deep red patterns from her ankles to her thighs that would last all night after she took them off, as if she'd branded herself on purpose.

There with the man beneath the heat of the sun, as if continuing the discussion of her skin's delicacy, she felt her eyes dazzle, dizzying her. She lifted her gaze. The sun's enormity bore down upon her, its brightness lighting up the whole sky. Her head spun, yet she found herself enchanted by the effect.

The hat did little to relieve the heat. The shadow cast by its brim covered only her forehead, leaving her nose exposed. Light and heat poured from the sky like boiling water, splitting over her head as it followed the lines of her body on its way to the ground.

"Look—it's true! There really are no shadows at noon!"

The woman drew up short, staring down at her feet as she spoke.

And indeed, all that was visible at her feet, and at the man's feet as well, was the incandescent white of the concrete.

"I remember as a child being fascinated by how I couldn't throw a shadow at noon. How silly! But I can't help but think of it now."

The woman knew she was talking only to herself, and when the man began walking again without answering her, she started walking too.

The woman had the urge to rattle the man, shake him up a little as he marched so patiently onward. What was he thinking about? The woman, for her part, was thinking about how if they only had a room, they'd be alone together right now. Was he thinking the same thing, just not putting it into words? Were the two of them walking through this bright expanse, exposed on all sides, the very opposite of what they'd come here for, each thinking separately about the time they should be spending together in their own private chamber?

"In any case, we might as well go all the way to the end. There might be a breeze there."

The man finally spoke. His heavy, dark-colored trousers looked horribly hot in the sun.

"Is there anywhere we could sit for a moment?"

"Even if there were any trees, there wouldn't be shade."

"Oh, I'm so thirsty."

As she spoke, the woman felt everything around her melt together, the line dividing the sea from the sky dissolving in the too-bright light.

"Didn't you just have a cola? Or two?"

The man's words reminded the woman that she had indeed indulged—perhaps overindulged—in some refreshments at the wharf's concession stand.

"If we're going to be walking like this, I'll be thirsty no matter how much I drink!" she insisted. *Thirsty.* The word echoed through her body.

"There might be a coffeeshop or something. We can check when we get back."

The man continued walking single-mindedly along the concrete path as if nothing in the world interested him more than whatever lay ahead.

"Why do we have to go all the way to the end?"

The woman feared that this arduous trip up and down the length of the breakwater would leave her bright red. The combination of the salt-laden air and the sizzling sun threatened to burn her to a crisp.

"Standing around is even more horrible," said the man sullenly.

"More horrible?"

She repeated his words back to him even as it occurred to her that what made things *even more horrible* for him may in fact be her.

She began to hear music up ahead. Out to the left of the breakwater, several fishing boats bobbed in the sea, eye-catchingly painted in shades of white and red and yellow. The paint looked fresh. Why? Was the fishing business going so well? Their presence bothered the woman. All these bright boats crowded together, their vivid primary colors jostling for her attention as if to provoke her. She could hear the music more clearly now. She could also see three or four young men, seemingly from the city, reclining on the deck of one of the boats. The music was coming from their radio. Rock music. The young men wore flashy shirts in the same colors as the paint on the boats.

"Listening to rock music, in this heat…"

The woman looked over at the boats as she spoke to the man.

Perhaps responding to her look, the young men all fixed their gazes on the woman at once. Their eyes followed her and the man as they continued their walk along the breakwater. Even the ones who'd been lying flat on the deck raised their heads to stare at them passing by.

Rock music, in this heat—the woman rolled the words around in her mouth, repeating them without quite saying them aloud.

Hot Day

Here, on this searingly white beach, with not even the slightest hint of a cool breeze, the music blasted like a hot wind. It covered the area with the sticky, nauseating smell of these young men's vitality, their greasy life force dancing out from the center of their very existence, perpetually on the verge of violence, ready to strike out at everything around them.

"Hey! Missus! Or should I say Miss? Hey!"

Voices came from the boat.

The voices appeared like a planned part of their walk to the pier. They hailed her like a threat turned proposition, or a proposition turned threat.

The voices continued.

"You two are lookin' for a place to go, ain't that right? Ain't it?"

A place to go? The woman muttered the words to herself. It occurred to her that this may indeed be why the man insisted on taking her on this long walk to the end of the pier. No room at the inn, so they needed another place. And that place might as well be this piece of hot, white concrete they were standing on, so bright it blotted out both sea and sky.

"Look at those red pants—they're split in the back! Right in two! Your ass is hanging out! Everyone can see except you! Poor Miss! Or Missus?"

The voices followed them even as they left the boats behind.

The woman lagged a step behind the man, her legs lethargic. It seemed to her that the man had been silent for a while now. But perhaps the man felt the same about her. The voices of the young men clung to their shared silence like a hallucination.

"It's like torture."

The woman's voice was soft.

"Indeed."

The man answered in a way that suggested that he may not have grasped the woman's meaning.

"Why are you making us walk down this hot path?"

The woman finally asked what she'd been meaning to ask all along.

"Look—we're here."

The man pointed. And then he walked the rest of the way without her.

The two of them stood at the end of the pier and looked around, seeing what they could see.

"There's no wind."

The woman removed the man's hat from her head, using it to shade her eyes. The ever-present light reflecting off the unmoving sea pierced them anyway. The light entered her pupils and filled her body with its shrill buzz like a cloud of cicadas.

"It's nice to be able to see out in the distance like this."

The man spoke as if unable to perceive anything beyond his own preconceptions.

"Nothing out here looks distant."

The woman knew the man's habits of thought; she was trying to provoke him.

"Off that way, you can see where the sky splits open. It all starts opening up there. Or at least, that's how you can think of it. Isn't it better that way? Better than not seeing an opening at all?"

"It seems like nothing more than a vast prison to me. The sea, the sky—everything's closed tight."

The woman spoke forcefully.

And she spoke the truth. The woman felt trapped, even as she wasn't trying to flee. The sky was no blue expanse traversed by wind; the sea was no whitecap-dotted azure plain. Everything was the same color, as if metal—silver? lead? tin?—had been melted down and poured over every surface. *And here I am*, thought the woman, *trapped in the center of this shining, sealed dome.*

"Shall we go back?" asks the man.

"And then go where?"

The woman couldn't help but contemplate how unendurable it would be to head right back the way they'd come.

The man raised his hand to indicate the way. The woman

turned to look. Which meant she was looking at where she'd just been from the opposite direction. The breakwater they'd walked along stretched out before her, and then beyond it, the town in apparent slumber. Everything shone pure white. The woman realized for the first time then that a landscape could be shadowless. It wasn't simply because it was noon. Everything before her exuded light without throwing the slightest shadow. An eerily still surface beneath which life seethed and roiled, an invisible vortex twisting ever more into itself.

The man began to walk, and the woman followed.

In the brief period between when they'd first set out for the pier and now, the concrete seemed to have become even hotter. Heat transmitted through the soles of her sandals with every step she took. *At least I'm walking*, she thought. *If I stood still, it would be like standing on a hot, flat griddle.*

"All I can think about right now are memories from my childhood. When we'd go to the beach, we'd run across the sand to swim, and it was so hot we had to keep hopping from foot to foot or it would burn us!"

The soles of the shoes she was wearing now seemed no different from the soles of her bare feet then.

The man didn't answer.

"But back then, we had the sea to run to—we could stand

anything, since we knew that sweet relief was just ahead. Unlike now."

The woman emphasized these last words in particular.

Being continually conscious of the heat felt like self-abuse. It was as if her body were no more than a layer of thin skin barely containing a molten core of pure heat. She felt heavy with its smolder and longed for the release of bursting into flame.

Why?

She asks herself.

Because there was no room at the inn.

She answers.

But maybe that wasn't it at all. Maybe she's been walking with the man through the heat since long before, and will continue to long after—she imagined herself walking on a hot day with him forever.

The woman began to sense something bearing down on them from the right, and she turned her head to look. The young men were there again, staring at them from the boat. But unlike before, they said nothing, content to let their gazes assert their presence for them.

Exposed.

The word came to the woman's mind.

She felt as though everything about her was exposed to the gaze of others. The woman tore the man's hat from her head and waved it in the air as if to ward off the young men's eyes. She longed to enlist the man's aid. But he was exposed too, after all; they were trapped in this exposure as long as they walked this path.

Why did the young men refrain from calling after them this time? Their silent gazes drew attention to the abject shame of the man and the woman walking together even more than the humiliating words they'd shouted before.

"Horrible."

The woman murmured the word to herself.

Horrible.

The word seemed to bounce off the young men and echo within her.

The white, shadowless concrete stretched wordlessly on before them. The woman continued to walk with the man along its length. The fishing boats receded from view, the gazes of the young men dissipating into the glittering air with them, leaving the woman alone with the heaviness of her body to carry like a burden with every step. Was the sunbaked concrete exuding breath like an expanse of grass would? Something rose from it like a heat shimmer, a wet smell like steam threatening to suffocate her.

"Time just refuses to pass sometimes, doesn't it?"

They'd reached the wharf again when the man said this.

It was still only one o'clock. Still two and a half hours until the boat arrived at three-thirty.

"What should we do?" the woman asked with a sigh.

"Should we take a little walk that way?"

The man pointed at the coastline that lay in the opposite direction from where they'd just been.

"Another walk?" asked the woman, but the man had already started on his way, leaving her little choice but to follow.

It was true, though—there was nothing to do but walk. There didn't seem to be a café or anywhere else to sit down, and even if there was, the woman imagined herself sitting on a greasy seat in the kind of café a fishing village like this might have and grew even more dispirited.

As they followed the curve of the coastline, the streets of the little town gradually fell away, and they began to skirt past the foot of a small mountain. The fishing wharf had been built in one of the meager tracts of level land that could be found at the tip of this mountainous peninsula, opening out to the south and west. They had walked southbound to the end of the pier, and now they were walking westbound along the land's edge. It was as if they were following the path of the sun, as if the afternoon itself was opening up for them. The rough, searing glory of the midsummer afternoon spread its arms in welcome. Every surface opened up wide, completely exposed. The land they walked on was no more than the tilted slope between the mountain and the sea, and as they made their way across it, the sky merged with the water and hung heavily over them, as if on the verge of burying them like an avalanche.

"Oh, I should have had another cola back at the wharf!" exclaimed the woman, just remembering.

It no longer felt as though she were being showered in heat falling from the sky; rather, the heat without and the heat within had become continuous. The woman stopped and looked up. For a moment, she had the impression that the unbearable summer heat was simply the surplus her body couldn't manage to contain flooding out from her into the sky.

"Look, there's a trail over there. You want to follow it?" asked the man.

And in fact, he'd already stepped one foot onto the little trail that branched off the main road along the coastline and led straight up the slope itself.

Lacking any better idea for what to do, the woman went along with the man's suggestion. Soon, shortness of breath accompanied the stifling heat. They climbed higher and higher with every step. The smell of burnt soil rose from their feet. The sun beat down on this place all day long, turning the soil into fine, dry powder.

"Oh, tangerines!"

The woman raised her eyes at the man's words.

About midway up the slope lay a tangerine orchard. The trail ran right along its edge. Shrunken and small-limbed, the tangerine trees threw no shade to speak of. Yellow woven mats were spread here and there beneath them, but the woman noticed that the bright yellow of these seemingly brand-new mats reflected the sun intensely, sizzling there beneath the trees.

"Gosh, I wonder what those are for?"

Hearing the man, a strange feeling overcame the woman. Could he be insisting on walking all over like this because he was still looking for a place to go? These mats looked just big enough, after all.

"Let's go back down. There's nothing here."

The woman turned her back to the mountain.

The sun, now slightly lower in the sky, had transformed the water's surface into a sea of scales. Each one shone bright, a mass of individual steel plates. She felt them fill her field of vision, overwhelming her. She was a tiny dot in the landscape, the glittering world bearing down upon her like the point of a funnel.

The man and the woman reached where the trail had branched off, then continued along the main road in the same direction they'd been walking before. The curve of the coastline meant that when they looked behind them, the wharf was no longer visible.

"I wonder how long this road goes?"

The woman didn't really care about the answer to her question, but she posed it anyway.

"I don't know—let's keep going and see what happens."

The man's voice was calm as always. What was he really thinking?

Let's go, let's go. It had been the man who'd insisted from the beginning. And it was true that there was really nothing else to do around here until three-thirty finally rolled around. But where was there to actually go? This sunbeaten slope by the sea. This winding little road, barely wide enough for a cart to pass. This dry, red soil that puffed up with every step. However long they walked, however far, that's all there was, it seemed.

"It's so hot."

The woman felt like she'd run out of anything else to say.

"Yeah, it really is."

The man seemed to feel the same way as he agreed.

The road took another turn, revealing a group of bathers. They seemed to be residents of the little fishing village, a few groups of adults and children playing around in the sea more than truly swimming in it. Several rocks jutted up here and there in the shallow water, the rocky bottom clearly visible. There were three small huts standing near the beach as well.

Were they the dwellings of villagers who'd elected to live away from everyone else?

The sound of rubber flip-flops slapping the ground approached from behind: *peta, peta, peta, peta.*

The woman turned to look and saw two young men, seemingly villagers, walking toward her. They were both tall with tanned, husky physiques, their steps forceful as they strode along. Their features struck her as countrified, but the men were also oddly fashionable, what with their modishly long hair and sunglasses.

The young men passed the man and the woman, and as they did, a glint of light from their sunglasses struck the woman's eye like a bright wink, and her nose was assaulted by the prickling smell of their armpits.

Right then, a little girl of around four or five, dressed in all red, emerged from one of the huts and began to toddle across the beach toward the road.

Seeing her, the two young men quickened their pace to a run. The body odor she'd smelled before trailed after them, hanging stickily in the air and making her head spin. The young men were upon the little girl in an instant. They ripped the clothing from her body in the blink of an eye, both top and bottom. Her plump flesh exposed completely, the little girl's mouth opened wide like a frog's, allowing the woman to see all the way inside; she seemed to be screaming. Yet, for some reason, the woman couldn't hear her screams at all. The young men each grabbed one of the girl's legs, spreading them to expose the pink within. The woman saw every fleshy fold as if looking through a magnifying glass. The two young men lifted the girl by the legs and threw her in the air once, then twice, then three times, flipping her in the air with every throw. Then they threw her to the ground and leapt upon her.

"Aaah!"

The man raised his right hand, pointing.

"Did you—?"

The woman turned to look hard at the man.

Then the woman returned her gaze to the scene before her. She blinked, then blinked again. The two young men in sunglasses were making pleasant conversation with an adult woman who'd emerged from one of the huts; she seemed to be the little girl's mother. The little girl herself, dressed in her red outfit, jumped and played around them, happy as could be.

The woman looked hard again at the man.

"What were you about to say?"

"Oh, nothing—I was mistaken."

The man started walking ahead again.

The woman followed him like always. She wanted to ask if he'd seen the same hallucination she had, but the heat had exhausted her to the point where doing anything at all, including putting the thought into words, seemed entirely too much trouble.

As they passed the huts, the woman couldn't help but stare hard at the young men, the woman, and the little girl as they socialized near the entrance of one of the huts, prompting them, in turn, to look back at her with naked suspicion.

The road continued to follow the curve of the coastline, and soon the huts disappeared from view behind them. They walked ever westward, following the sun's path as if intentionally trying to remain in the shadowlessness directly beneath it. There were no longer any buildings or trees; the only life was the sun itself.

"It's finally starting to set."

With those words, the woman took the man's hat from her head and raised it up in the air to block the sun. She started walking again. Her arm quickly grew tired. The shadow thrown by the alignment of the sun and the hat protected only her head. It did nothing to prevent her arms and torso and legs from burning. Everywhere her skin showed was already reddening. Still, the woman persevered in her effort to block at least a portion of the sun's rays, and she continued walking with her left arm jutting up at an angle, the man's hat clutched in her fist.

The woman realized then that the clothes she was wearing were the same red as those worn by the little girl. She didn't share her realization with the man, however, continuing instead to walk with him down the hot path.

砂の檻

Cage of Sand

Taeko Kono

Translated by Lucy North

Cage of Sand

"Oi!" she heard as she was making her way across a crosswalk. Glancing back, she raised her eyes and saw a pickup truck coming out of a side street behind her. "Get a move on, will you! Walk!" The driver pounded the windowsill of his cab.

She looked over at the other side of the road. It was a sunny day, and the walk sign was difficult to discern, but she was certain it was still green. Even if it was flashing, there would still be a little time before it turned red. All she had to do was get across before then.

Feigning obliviousness, she continued walking across the road, which most other pedestrians had now finished crossing, without quickening her pace in the slightest. Reaching the curb, she looked up at the walk sign, and confirmed it was flashing. The pickup truck completed its turn and sped away.

Get a move on, will you! Walk! How rude! And disrespectful! What a thing to say to a person… Only after walking a whole block did she think up a retort. *You have brakes, don't you? Use them!* That would have been pleasingly pointed, yet casual. In the moment, though, she hadn't even had the presence of mind to reflect that she should avoid having anything to do with the man: she'd simply done her utmost to avert her gaze, in anger and shock. Of course, even if the words had occurred to her, she wouldn't have uttered them, but the length of time it had taken her to come up with even that reply showed how shocked and angered she had been. She was still hot and flustered, and showing it, she could tell. Realizing that something about her demeanor had irritated the man to the point of yelling at her, she grew even hotter.

She had alighted from the bus and was waiting for the lights at the crosswalk when she happened to glance back at the police box and became absorbed in what was going on.

A police officer stood guard in the doorway chatting with some children, all a similar age and height.

"Is that a child? Or a grown-up?" one of the children was asking.

"Hm. Good question," the officer replied.

On the lower half of the glass door of the police box was a poster with a sketch of a man wanted in connection with the murder of a bar hostess. The figure in the sketch had the look of a youth who liked to spend his time walking idly around town.

"Is that a grown-up?" another child pressed.

"It'd be bad news if he was a child." That was the officer, joking. "Yes, he's a grown-up."

"He doesn't look like a grown-up."

"He's a bit short, apparently—like a child."

"Where's he from?"

"Nobody knows."

"Nobody knows? How come?"

"Well, nobody's seen him."

"But how could they draw him, if nobody's seen him?"

"A few people have seen him, probably. But only a very few."

The man's age—*Approximately 35*—had been crossed out with a red marker and corrected to *Approximately 45*.

"Hey. You're being called."

The officer pointed to a woman a few yards down the street who was throwing glances back at the children, and away they dashed. But she for her part had remained, her eyes drawn to the poster. She could understand why the children were puzzled. The man looked bizarre: a bit like a dwarf. But in addition to his short stature, there was something else about this youth who liked to spend his time walking idly around town. He had the look, she realized, of a youth who had reached adulthood without changing in any way whatsoever. She became aware that people were now surging across the crosswalk, and she too began to cross, still ruminating on this youth who had reached adulthood without changing in any way whatsoever, and then that rude shout had come from the pickup truck. The anger she felt was likely due to her shock, but she wouldn't have been so shocked had any other thought been on her mind.

Someone had once told her something about people with intellectual disabilities: that they go from childhood directly into old age. The exact point that they go from one to the other is unpredictable, varying from person to person, but in each case, after a childhood that has lasted far too long, they are, all too suddenly, very old indeed. As someone who had cause to wonder about people who'd reached adulthood without changing in any way whatsoever, she considered this something worth remembering. It had recently been on her mind quite a bit.

Whenever, for example, she took the lid off a canister of roasted seaweed she'd thought was full and discovered that it was depleted, only one or two strips at the bottom, she would be reminded of those people. As she would be anytime a sudden shower of rain made her hurry to bring in bedding that she had hung out to air.

If anything, she felt envy for people who could suddenly become very old indeed. She was middle-aged, a stage of life that they would never have to endure.

And her age in the sexual realm? What age was she there?

It'd be bad news if he was a child. Yes, he's a grown-up. The police officer's words rang in her ears. She was aware that she was getting flustered all over again. She remembered the suspect's height: *150 cm.* To an observer, that might not seem so very different from her own. But the range given for his age—written in first as *Approximately 35,* then *Approximately 45...* The range for her age in the sexual realm had to be much wider—certainly more than ten, maybe twenty years, maybe even more. Where should she place herself? She tried one place and then another, haphazardly, but it was impossible: the more she tried, the more impossible it became.

Nobody knows?

Well, nobody's seen him.

But how could they draw him, if nobody's seen him?

A few people have seen him, probably. But only a very few.

That too would apply to her, she thought. It wasn't as if, in her own situation, she was completely unseen. But she had been seen by only a very few.

*

"So he said to take all of these?" her husband asked when she got home, taking the bundle she extracted from her shopping bag and squeezing it in both hands.

"I imagine that's what he means."

Taking the bundle back, she opened it up. Five paper prescription packets stuffed with medicaments, in clear plastic bags. Two packets of antibiotics with detailed instructions; a remedy for the common cold with merely the dose noted; a medicine to ease digestion; and some vitamins for tiredness and fatigue. This was still only the third trip her husband had taken abroad, but he was always gone for a very long time. He was in perfectly good health, and yet he had taken to asking a pharmacist friend to assemble a set of medicines in the unlikely event that he fell ill.

"Look. These I don't need." Her husband set aside the vitamins. "It's up to me anyway. Got to draw the line somewhere. You can have them. As payment for house-sitting. The rest can go in the little room."

The little room, which once would have been occupied by a maid, was being used as the staging area for his trip. At one point there had been so many things strewn over the floor, there was barely room to stand. It was somewhat tidier now. The suitcase they had decided to pack with only those things that he was certain to take was filled to the brim. They were now putting things onto its open flap, which they'd propped up using a lower drawer from the wooden storage chest.

Atop the chest lay a pencil and an unfolded cigarette pack on which she had written a list of the items that he had to take, and those he wanted to take if room allowed. Items that had been dealt with were marked with a circle, while those he had decided against had a line drawn through them. Now she could put a circle beside *Medicines*. At this point there weren't many items left to deal with, and the same seemed to be true of the list of errands her husband had kept for himself—he appeared to be using some kind of notebook. For the last ten days, he had been intensely busy with all sorts of tasks, which he'd begun all at once, but now, finally, it seemed he'd reached the homestretch. She had absolutely no recollection of the first thing that her husband had done this year in anticipation of his trip abroad. She had a clear memory of what he'd done last year. Last year, like this year, he had decided to go away at the start of spring, but last year, once the decision had been made, before any other task, he had reinforced the house's closed-board fence.

They were only renting their current house, but it had been built before the war as a private residence, and it was well constructed. The slatted fence and the low gate at the front looked strong and must have been replaced at some point. The closed-board fence at the back of the house, however, was in a dilapidated state, and she could only assume it was the original. The materials and construction were good, but there were now so many broken boards and split rails that had been left unrepaired that the whole thing slanted: it was remarkable it stood up at all. The boards, rails, posts, and supports had turned green, and most of the concrete bases seemed to have crumbled, so that whenever a strong typhoon came, the posts would pop out and the entire fence, which ran the length of the garden, would lean—but even so, it always remained in one piece; it never truly collapsed, or fell apart. After each typhoon, she and her husband would ease the posts back into the holes, and the fence would resume its shape once more. They would never have guessed, had they not lived there, that the fence was in such a weakened state.

Pretty early on, they'd realized, after seeing a cat try to walk atop it, that it was a fence that would tip this way and that. One or two neighborhood cats had tried to leap onto it only to be flung straight off.

"Burglars will never get over that," her husband remarked. "A weak fence may well be safer than a strong one."

Last year, in the spring, they'd had a snowfall, but putting this task before all others now he'd decided to go, her husband had placed a stepstool next to the fence where there were still lingering patches of snow, and, moving it from one spot to another, used planks and netting to tether sections that looked particularly precarious to nearby trees.

The house was a bungalow, built with a mix of Japanese and Western elements: none of the windows had storm shutters, and it had a lot of shrubs and trees. It looked wide open to intruders, and in fact so it proved to be. Soon after they'd moved in, a loquat tree in the backyard started to bear fruit, and one day after leaving the house for a few hours, she came back to find skins and seeds scattered on the ground. It didn't look like the work of birds, and she was mystified. A few days later, she arrived home to voices, one of them her husband's. Thinking he must have come home early, perhaps with a colleague, she went into a room to find her husband standing on the engawa. He glanced back at her.

"I came home to find these intruders, stealing our loquats." Turning back, he ordered: "Write down your school year and your homeroom number."

Two small boys were crouching below him in the garden, each clutching a pencil. Heads almost touching, they were writing on scraps of paper, which he must have given them, resting them on his old geta.

"How did you get in?" her husband demanded.

"Well, we used the tree out front to get up onto the shed," one of the boys explained, down on his hands and knees, waving his pencil in the air. "Then we got up onto the little roof of the kitchen…"

The following fall, a burglar broke in. It happened when the evenings were starting to darken slightly earlier, on a day when there'd been sporadic showers. By the time she got home, though she hadn't meant it to be so late, the house was shrouded in darkness.

As soon as she entered the living room, she saw in an instant, even in the gloom, that there were mounds of stuff all over the floor, and switching on the light, she was met with what looked like the aftermath of a riot. A few seconds later, she realized the window was ajar—the garden was in full view. Shutting it, she discovered that the frosted glass near the latch was shattered. She should check the other rooms. The guest room was unscathed, but one of the glass doors of the engawa was wide open. Somebody had once told her that thieves only start their work after first devising a getaway route. The other three rooms were all untouched. The thief had probably left seconds before through this prepared exit, hearing her come in. Well, thank goodness he had. The thought of coming face-to-face with a stranger in her house who might have asked what she was doing there made her feel faint.

In the case of the two boys, they had let them leave, discarded the pieces of paper, and forgotten the incident, but with the burglar she and her husband, who returned home soon after her, contacted the local police. Two officers came and distributed silver powder over all the surfaces in the house with fine brushes, dusting for fingerprints. They found several, but they all turned out to be hers. Underneath the sea of clothing on the floor, she discovered her wallet, normally kept in her miniature set of drawers. She opened it to find it, predictably, empty. The first-aid box, even the package of new bed linen a friend had recently sent her to celebrate her recovery from an illness, had been opened and searched, for good measure. But her small change purse that she kept on a shelf in the kitchen cabinet, right behind a frosted glass door, had been left alone.

"People don't generally keep their valuables behind glass," one of the police officers explained.

Her husband had taken his first trip abroad two years ago. They'd been living in another house at the time.

"When you turn off the main road, you see it right there," she would say, when giving directions to that first house. "A house sticking up out of nowhere." This wasn't strictly true, but it appeared that way because once you turned off the main road, the street split in two: one leading to a row of shops, and the other to a parking lot owned by their landlord and a house with a sizeable lawn. Their house, a single residence with two floors, was situated between the parking lot and the lawn.

"The size of a postage stamp" was how her husband, whose work was somewhat architecture related, liked to describe that house. It had no bathroom. Entry was via the kitchen. It was square shaped, with two rooms on each floor. A stair ladder went up the center. The view from the windows on three sides was unobstructed, but there was no garden, just a perimeter wall, made of cinder blocks, that extended off the front of the house. Every window and every door that opened onto a veranda was fitted with tin-covered storm shutters. When she and her husband went out in the evening they would close the shutters, and the first thing they'd see on their return would be their little dwelling, all locked up, looking like a solitary oil drum.

It was only once they'd moved to their present house that it became clear how protected from outside incursion that first house had been. While there, they hadn't even been conscious of it being safe, and their life had passed without a single untoward incident. If anything, they had encouraged a breach themselves.

On summer nights her husband would bolt the gate, place a wooden tub on the path, and take a quick wash in the open air. One evening, she could hear him throwing pailfuls of water over himself—he was clearly planning on going out to drink—when he called for her.

"It would have been easy enough to put a board there," he said, pointing to the foot of the wall by the path. At certain sections, the cinder blocks had grates for ventilation. Sand was spilling in through them.

"It's the same there," he said. She looked at the next section of the wall. "We can't let this go—it's not right. More and more of it is pouring in." He touched it with a finger, producing a small avalanche.

When she went out to the road to dispose of the water from the tub, she noticed a mountain of sand lodged against the other side of the wall. It was going to be used to fill in the potholes in the paved parking lot next door.

On his return later that night, her husband told her, his shoes still on, to come outside. "Do you have something I can poke with?" he added. "Maybe a disposable chopstick." She suspected he might be a little inebriated, but he squatted down by one of the grates in the wall and used the chopstick to encourage the sand to pour in onto the path.

"He shouldn't have just left it there," he said, meaning the landlord. "This house does belong to him. We can take some."

She squatted too, a little way along. Copying him, she placed the tip of a chopstick in a grate, and worked it back and forth, and sure enough the sand came through. In the center of the path, where people trod, were some square stepping stones, made of cinder blocks buried in the ground, no doubt left over from when the wall was built. Water collected in the hollows after his baths, and after rain. His idea was to use the sand to even out the ground.

"I wonder what he'll say when he next drops by," she said, as she moved her chopstick back and forth.

"If anything, he should thank us. For carrying out home improvements. This sand..."

"—Hush, dear...."

"You think I care?" he continued, loud as before. "This sand has slipped through our barrier. There's no stopping sand. May as well not be a wall here at all."

*

Over the last year, she had started to feel uncertain about the system of netting and planks attached to the trees that her husband had rigged up to prevent the old fence from collapsing into the neighbor's yard or into their own. The netting had stretched, even ripped, in places; and a few planks had come out and were hanging uselessly from the trees. The sections that held together were the exception rather than the rule.

When her husband went out into the yard early in the morning; when he suddenly got to his feet, casting his newspaper aside; when he came home early in the day and buttoned up a clean shirt in preparation to go out again that evening—she would wait, sure that the next thing he'd say would be:

"Well, I should get to work and fix up our tattered little fence."

But instead, he would complain: "How long are you planning to hang on to this box of rice husks?" Or else he would announce, strapping on his watch: "I'm going out. I'll be home late." Or he would head straight to his own room.

She could not help doubting whether it would even occur to him to work on the old fence before he went away. Would he ever get around to it?

"How time flies! A week from today I'll be off."

Hearing him announce this as he stood looking at the calendar, she observed his profile and tried to read what was going through his mind.

If the fence did collapse during his absence, she was confident, without knowing why, that she would be able to handle it on her own. And she didn't like thinking that his indifference to repairing the fence was a sign of his indifference to her. There had been any number of times when he'd shown that he could be considerate—much more so than simply attending to a fence prior to going away on a trip. And yet, he could also be brutally inconsiderate—in ways that made his half-hearted interest in, even total indifference to, the fence insignificant by comparison.

Well, whatever he did—whether he remembered the fence and reinforced it, whether he left saying he had intended to but hadn't gotten around to it, whether he simply told her that this year it didn't need to be done, even if he left without acknowledging the fence at all—she would accept that her husband had his reasons, and was unconditionally right.

Yet despite being so philosophical, both about her husband and about the fence, it bothered her to think that it might be left completely untended. Even with last year's repairs, it was clearly in a dilapidated state.

If this year, unlike last year, her husband left without making a single reference to the fence, would she be different while he was gone? And if she were, in what way? If he did repair the fence, would she end up doing what she'd done last year? As she ruminated, she became uneasy, and the uneasiness only mounted as the days went by. The only thing she could be sure of was that, for the first few days, she would be out of the house a lot, busy with several tasks he had entrusted to her. That aspect, at least, would be exactly the same.

*

They sometimes went together to Haneda Airport to greet or see off friends. But he never asked her to go with him when he went to the airport at the start of his trip, or to meet him when he returned. And she never suggested it. He simply telephoned her just before he boarded, or just after he touched down.

Last year, she had taken his final call before takeoff from the bath. It was still early evening. She was lying in the tub using the gas hot-water heater, having placed the telephone near the bathroom door. When the telephone rang, she made sure to switch off the heating system before she picked up. If he heard the noise, he would only assume that she had seized the chance to lie around taking it easy.

Her husband chatted about this and that from the depths of the receiver as she held it in her wet hand, and then added, "Well, take care." That was it. He'd said the same thing earlier when he had left the house.

Those seemingly simple words might contain any number of meanings, she was aware, but she was aware too—whether she chose to listen, or not to listen, or only later recalled them—that they would never change. Nevertheless, the simplicity, and the fact that he had said them to her twice, made her suspect that he might be referring to something that only seemed to be one thing, but was in fact several conjoined ones. She lay in the hot water, letting the words become engorged, pressing and prodding them.

As she pressed intently around an area she thought most likely to yield, it wasn't long before something started to loosen. She worked at it a little, and it came away. Taking it in her hand, she felt a chuckle rise in her throat.

Why choose to repair the fence right then? Just days before leaving?

When she'd first spotted her husband in the yard fixing up the fence, her first reaction had been mild surprise. "Good gracious!" It was the surprise of a woman who was just coming around to accepting that her husband, who usually did no more than get her to help prop up the fence when it leaned over or popped out anyway, was about to go off, leaving her without a second thought. She had not actually told her husband about her feeling that something really quite untoward might take place in the house during that long period that she was on her own, though in truth she was thinking that as soon as he left, she must go straight out to buy a few more locks. But to judge from the fact that he was mending the fence, her husband might well have been conscious of it anyway. Though she fully understood that her husband had his reasons, and was unconditionally right, her surprise had also been about their matched concern.

Perhaps when he told her to *take care*, her husband was not speaking in general terms after all, but only pretending to do so, and was, underneath those words, referring specifically to the potential for that untoward something. The fact that he had avoided referring to the fence, and in fact anything related to it, could well be because he had sensed that she was anxious about it, and wanted to avoid making her more so. Suddenly, a strong anxiety gripped her.

For several days after her husband's departure, she made excursions out of the house, intent on tackling the errands her husband had left for her to do. And, having decided that she would make sure that the doors and windows of the house were as secure as possible, on her way home she would stop off at her local hardware store to purchase as many locks as she could carry. Sometimes she would only be home for a few minutes before deciding she wanted yet another lock for yet another place, and she would set out immediately to buy it.

"What on earth do you want with so many?" the young clerk asked. She was at a loss for a reply. Wrapping up two sets, each with two padlocks inside, he was clearly referring to her frequent visits. The same clerk had already served her several times before.

"Oh. Um, well, it's my brother, you know," she finally managed to say. "He wants the whole lot of them. They use all sorts of strange things these days for art. Sticking on bits of wood and cast iron… That's what he does."

But, she thought, she had inquired too specifically about the way the locks worked to be buying them as art materials. Why hadn't she thought to buy a few at a time at different stores? As it was, she may as well have gone there expressly to tell that store clerk that she was going to be a woman living alone, for probably half a year, in a house where something really quite untoward might occur. No sooner had her husband left than she had done this stupid thing, concerning the very matter about which she had to *take care*.

Panicked, she went home brooding and lost no time in scribbling a note to put in the milk crate by the front gate. She had written a note on the day her husband departed with instructions to cut delivery of milk by one bottle, but it occurred to her now that it would be safer to arrange for delivery of two bottles again, even if she couldn't drink both, and to have her local wine merchant deliver a bottle of sake and beer occasionally.

It wasn't unusual for her to find herself sleeping alone even when her husband was around: he would sometimes stay out all night. On such nights, as someone who if anything preferred late nights, she would often find herself preparing for bed at two or three in the morning, having become immersed in some task. Ordinarily, she felt forced to keep the same schedule as her husband, who liked to get up and go to bed early, at least when he was home. When she was sleeping on her own, she could go to bed with the knowledge that in a few hours it would be getting light, no one was going to break in now, but even that was almost secondary to the knowledge that she would be able to sleep in for as long as she liked in the morning. Twice during the past month, she had enjoyed sleeping in.

This was not, however, something that she wanted regularly, and besides, last year, even while he was away, though her schedule had gotten slightly later, she had still woken early in the mornings. Her eyes would snap open as if there were something important she had to do. Then, head on her pillow, she would gaze around her in astonishment. She'd been sleeping in a veritable fortress. The single fusuma that formed a partition to the guest room was blocked by her desk, which was stacked with books to the top of the wooden doorframe. Each of the two diamond-paned panels of the serving hatch in the wall between the room and the kitchen had a guard lock on its upper and lower ledges to stop it being slid sideways or raised. There were similar locks fixed to the top and bottom of the frame of the front door of the house, which also had a pole propped against it for extra security—it would have to be removed for her to leave. The reason that the room felt oppressive, like a fortress, was no doubt because of all the curtains.

She got out of bed and opened them, revealing an array of security locks attached to the tops and bottoms of the frosted-glass panes. The two sliding screens inside one window—the one through which the burglar had made his entry that time—and the four inside the other window were fastened with auxiliary locks and security locks screwed right through the wood at the top and bottom. Wanting to let in some fresh air, she tried to open the screen, but it only moved as far as the locks allowed. She opened two separate screens partway and stood by the window, casting her eyes over the view outside.

Directly in front of her was the paulownia tree, its trunk wrapped in netting attached to the fence behind it. The image of her husband standing on the stepstool he'd placed beside the fence, where there'd still been some lingering patches of snow, bending back to view first the fence and then the tree, then pulling the netting tighter, rose in her mind's eye. It was just as if he were preparing to keep her cooped up—like a pet. Remembering the scene, she wondered if being cooped up had changed her into someone whose whole existence was defined by that condition.

Far from allaying her anxiety, the precautions she took only heightened it. The house was not large, less than thirty tsubo in area; and yet, even after locking herself in with enough locks to fill an entire bucket (as she would discover later), plus window bars, desk, books, stones, and steel wire, she was still coming across places she had overlooked.

The window casing in the little room was thin, the two upper panes of glass transparent. The lock was far too big for the frame, surely visible from outside. It would take no time for an intruder to break the glass, locate a weak place in the wood with his hands, and rip the lock off. She suddenly recalled the burglary. The burglar was still at large. What if she were to use

Scotch tape to secure the lower panes of the window to the bottom of the frame, sealing it up along the edges and where the upper and lower panes met in the middle? She didn't need to use this window. If someone did try to open it, the tape would make a sound. Yes, she thought, and hurried out to buy Scotch tape. One by one, other places around the house got sealed up.

Now that she was spending so much time on her own, she had been making the odd trip to the local public bath, and for a while she savored the pleasure, not having done so for two years. But then the effort of securing all the places that could never be fully secured prior to leaving began to outweigh the effort of drawing a bath, and she resumed taking her baths at home.

One day as she lay in her bath, she looked up at the little window and realized that this room was unsafe too. An average-sized man could easily push his way in: all he had to do was remove a single bar of the window's outer grille.

This window casing was even thinner than the one in the little room. Rather than a lock, here too, Scotch tape would do the trick. But that might put her at risk of gas poisoning. On the other hand, the steam might loosen the tape anyway. Either way, she had to do something. Such was the way her mind had operated, as she recalled.

And, as she recalled, barely a second or two later, she'd been struck by another thought. This was her chance. Such chances didn't come along every day. She had to do it. And do it now. Stepping into the dressing area, she stood before the cabinet mirror and repeated this to her own misting reflection. Then she opened the cabinet, snatched up her razor, and retreated into the bathroom once more.

It had sometimes occurred to her that the reason she was no longer seeing unsecured places was simply that she preferred not to, for her own peace of mind. And yet, it had never entered her head before now to carry out such a radical cosmetic treatment to this part of her body.

The sensation of the blade felt utterly strange. It took some skill to wield. She rinsed herself several times with hot water. She had convinced herself of the importance of seizing the moment, and she remained convinced. Was it the sense of a precious opportunity at her disposal that impelled the blade? Or the visible change wrought by each stroke of the blade that made her conscious of that preciousness? It was impossible to tell. Two or three times, she felt a coldness around her shoulders. The sense that the heat was leaving her along various parts of her body was distracting. When she felt chilled to the bone, she set the blade aside. Once done, she wondered if she had needed to worry quite so much. Then another, wholly unexpected thought struck her. Quite unintentionally, she had made a pledge of fidelity. She had made the coop even more impenetrable than it had been before.

*

The little room was now tidy and bare, her husband's four packed bags lined up neatly against the wall.

But at this point her husband returned to the house carrying a new trunk, made of steel. Hadn't he wanted to keep his baggage to a minimum? she asked. But this, he said, he intended to leave behind.

"If something happens and you have to stay somewhere else while I'm gone," he told her, "stow this trunk in the storage area under the kitchen floor."

She didn't understand. "What's inside it?" she asked.

"Hm? Oh, nothing much. Don't worry about it. I'm going to pack some of my stuff in it now. Work-related things, things that are important only to me. Nothing that concerns you. If it burns up, so be it. It's just that the storage area is safer than elsewhere in the house, and if I can keep these things safe, I'd like to. Just a precaution. But don't forget to bring the trunk out every now and again. It might look robust, but it won't keep out the damp." He continued, "It's possible, isn't it, you'll find yourself having to go away on a trip? You should go—why don't you? Don't you have pals you can go away with, just once? It's boring, isn't it, here on your own. What you need is a pet. But you don't like pets, do you. Well, what about a hobby? Six months is a long time!"

While he was speaking, she chimed in with "Yes," and "That's true." The first time he mentioned her taking a trip, he seemed to imply that she would be taking it out of necessity—which made her suspect that the trunk meant something significant. But then he changed tack, and made light of it all, as if to make her think that the trunk was not significant. Then he took the conversation in another direction entirely. She had a strong premonition that something she had not at all foreseen was about to occur.

So, when her husband said that six months was a long time, she nodded, and in an effort to elicit a little more information about this unforeseen something, she replied, with emphasis:

"Yes, that's true!"

At this, however, her husband headed to his own room, dragging the gleaming trunk behind him.

They were now midway through the week of his departure. Very likely, she thought, her eyes resting on the fence, it would receive no attention. For the next six months, it would remain completely untouched.

Last year during her husband's long absence, when on a sudden whim she'd brought the razor into the bathroom, and carried out that radical cosmetic treatment, then witnessed the way her body seemed so utterly changed, and realized that what she'd done was to construct the strongest possible pledge of fidelity, she had been shocked. But it wasn't the rashness of the act that had shocked her. True, she had felt a certain awkwardness at the way she had made the discovery. But really, it was infinitesimal. What's more, the treatment had indeed secured her fidelity. In addition to anticipation of the time when she would return to her former state, there seemed to have been an unconscious wish, not to prove that such a method would or would not work, but rather, in quiet protest, to show just how far she was prepared to go. And in that quiet protest was an inkling of optimism, she now understood, that the half-year break in her sex life would be just that, nothing more.

She'd had no idea, at that point, how long it would take her body to return to its former state. She had only done what she'd done in the knowledge that there was no possibility of its not returning to its former state by the time her husband came back in the fall. Nevertheless, she was glad that the idea had occurred to her so soon after he'd left, within days, rather than months, of his departure. It had been a matter of now or never.

She now knew that it took forty days. In reality, it was probably only roughly that, but forty days had come to mind, and she decided to use it as a way to remember. It might be worth doing so, just in case. On the other hand, it was also somewhat absurd.

In all likelihood, the keenness of the comfort she felt at the thought of forty days only seemed so because of the discomfort she habitually felt in not being able to know when, or if, they were going to have one of their primordial nights. The same logic surely underlay her enjoyment of the nights her husband spent out when he was at home—had she been single she wouldn't have enjoyed them. If, for the sake of argument, she'd been able to know that in forty days' time they would be having one of their primordial nights, the sense of comfort at the thought of a return to her original state, which would still have occurred with her husband home, would have been much less keen. And surely, the whole point of their nights was to know that they were going to come. If something happened that meant that they would never come again—well, the thought of forty days would have no meaning at all.

Their last such night had occurred when they'd just started to collect all the things he wanted to pack, in the now quite tidy and bare little room where his four packed bags were lined up against the wall.

In her excitement she had started to babble. "Dear, tell me what'll become of us…" When she babbled, they both became even more excited. The more desperately she implored him, the more sadistic her husband could be, or pretend to be. Which was just as she wanted. He would then start to tell her. Over and over again, endlessly. Each time he told her, she would ask to be told more. She was still the same woman she had always been since she had first become the woman whom only one or two people had ever seen, but at such times she would feel transported right back to the moment she had become that woman. And this too—why it should be—she would ask him to explain to her. And she would be aware of another self, situated slightly apart, like a musical accompaniment, begging for more.

The accompanying self wanted to be told that the day when their sex life would exhaust itself was still far off in the future; and that the consummation, when it came, would be the height of beauty. Also, that there was nothing wrong in dying for what they wanted—that the punishment that surely awaited them for daring to do such things was worth it.

The two parts accompanied each other in an exquisite melody. Even after the notes of the melody faded, becoming a mere reverberation, it played on in her ears. On and on, long after even the reverberation had ceased, and night had turned into day. It was like a melody in itself.

But rather than making her look forward to the next such night, the experience of having been transported back to herself—this self that only one or two people had ever seen—only left her even more anxious. It was already clear to her that the kind of love that she and her husband made, so different to that of most others, might exhaust itself sooner. To remember what they did was to become all the more conscious of its particularity—not only in what they did, but also for the effect it had on their relationship to time.

She could not imagine that in old age they would still be doing what they did now, tying each other up, playing at bondage, using ribbons, loosely, enjoying the kind of mood that this produced. Nevertheless, once that scene had popped up in her mind, she found it unbearably endearing. That was her hope—her ultimate ideal. The lovely tiny ideal shimmered like a golden charm way off in the distance. It would be impossible to attain it. The tiny golden speck seemed to her to be shining, the symbol of a perfect end. Even if it were forever out of her reach, she still wanted to bring things to completion in a way that was as much like it as she could manage. In the same way it helped to have a plan at the start of a journey, it would help to know what lay ahead. And yet, part of the essence of sex seemed to be that you could never be sure when or even if it would ever happen again.

That they had been able to share such a night so recently was no guarantee that another one would occur; and if it did, there was also no way to predict how it might unfold. If she'd known in advance that their most recent night would be their last (and as such, she would have liked to think, the last one of her life), she might then have been able to feel as if she had been given a share in the tiny golden speck of happiness that shone in front of her like a symbol of a perfect end. The knowledge that sex was now going to be irrelevant to her would have meant being set free from the cage. True, it was a cage of sand, one from which you could escape at any time if you so wanted. But the potential for escape was not the same thing as no cage at all. There was no way of making the cage inescapable, but it could make life extremely inconvenient. Overcoming the inconvenience, getting out of the cage, required wisdom and power—either one would have sufficed—but she had neither. Her lack of power was no doubt due to the considerable number of years that had passed since she had first become that woman whom only one or two people had seen. As for her lack of wisdom, perhaps she had yet to reach the age when one accrues such a thing.

For a woman who seemingly had lost power and had yet to develop wisdom, the cage was nothing but a nuisance. She wasn't conscious of any disgruntlement at the infrequency of their nights—she could not recall one instance when she herself had instigated anything. No, the reason she had become aware of the troublesome nature of the cage was because she dreaded what the long intervals might bring in their wake. Their unusual sex life meant that sometimes she felt ten years younger, but occasionally she felt ten years older, which was horrible to experience. She had begun to suspect that their unusual sexual activities were delaying the end of her youth, but also accelerating her toward old age. And the two weren't working against each other, but rather existed in one and the same place. During sex, if either one of the two processes got out of sync, whichever dominated would gain the decisively upper hand. If her explanation was correct, keeping both level might allow her to feel young for twice as long as other people, but also possibly make her age twice as fast—both in the sexual realm and in actuality.

Whether it was extended youth or sudden old age that won out, the extent of the victory did seem to her to be not unrelated to the length of the intervals between those nights. This was the reason that their infrequency made her fearful. It wasn't only old age winning that she feared. Youth was just as much cause for concern. For some reason, she felt that, if anything, it would be youth that would be the cause of her final collapse.

As the intervals dragged on, she found herself suspecting that her husband was purposely deferring their nights, to make her fret. But surely it was vital to limit such deferrals, in order to stave off a decisive victory for either youth or old age. This would both delay the ending—and mitigate it too. It would also allow her to get a clear sense, even if only fleetingly, of this middle-aged body of hers as it truly was.

In their unusual sex life, when she felt young, her husband seemed to experience the same intense feeling of youth; but when she felt old, he did not—he simply remained the age that he was in everyday life, while she was left to experience extreme old age by herself. As she waited out these long periods of neglect, she had sometimes wondered if the balance that she was eager to preserve was no longer there for the keeping. What kind of partner was a man who remained oblivious—who would become aware of the need to shore things up only when it was too late, who would only fix things after everything had tumbled down?

*

"Well, the expense of the journey is one thing," her husband had told her. "But commuting back and forth would exhaust me. If it were nearer, it might be convenient to come back regularly, but..." And he added: "You should try it. Stuffing yourself into a confined space for eighteen hours. You would get really fed up."

But there he was, going off again, content to be stuffed into a confined space for just such an amount of time. She had some idea of how uncomfortable it was from how he had behaved on his return last year—though she had little idea how he comported himself when he arrived at his destination, and she had to allow for a difference between a person arriving somewhere he'd expressly set off for, and returning to his place of departure.

Last year, on the day he was due back, she had risen early, removed the huge number of locks from around the house, peeled the Scotch tape off the doors and windows, and thoroughly cleaned the house, leaving the windows and sliding screens open. She gathered all the poles together and returned the stones to the yard.

The telephone call had come from Haneda Airport. Soon she had completed all her tasks. She calculated that it would be some time before he got back to the house. She'd stocked up the day before on supplies for supper, but there was one item she still needed, and she decided to take a chance and go out and purchase it. It wouldn't take ten minutes. For the first time in months, she dashed off leaving only the front door locked.

A car pulled into the end of their little road and came to a halt. Not her husband, surely. And yet, when she looked closer, she saw that it was. The door opened and the driver bounded out. Her husband seemed to have seen her, but he got out without acknowledging her and stood by the car. The driver went around to the back and the trunk sprang open.

"Where were you off to?" her husband asked her when she trotted up. The driver started to push a large, wheeled suitcase, carrying a bag in his other hand. Her husband had a heavy bag in either hand. She grabbed two bags. There were some other bags, which appeared to belong to him, but this would do for the time being. She followed the men back to the house.

"You've been well?" Her husband flung the question over his shoulder.

"Oh yes, very," she replied.

And then, just as she caught up with them, her husband said, "Come on! Unlock the door!" Turning to the driver, he said, in a mild tone, "Oh, just put them down there."

The driver went back to the car to collect more bags. Her husband went straight into the house, and immediately tsk-tsked his disapproval.

"What the hell?! You left every door and window in the house wide open!"

For two days after that, her husband scowled whenever she spoke to him, showing his irritation with every gesture and word. Then his mood changed, and he became cheerful. She could only assume that he had been curt with her because he had been so very tired.

*

In coaches there is often a space like a shelf behind the last row of seats. It gives the impression of offering only the smallest amount of space, but that is because the rear windshield slants up over it. It proves surprisingly capacious for storing pieces of baggage.

Her husband was lying diagonally across such a place, and she lay by his side.

"It's good we arrived early. We've got this great place all to ourselves."

"Yes, it would have been impossible now," she said. Or perhaps just thought. They lay there, stretched out on their backs. Beyond her feet, she could sense rows of seats, all already occupied, and more and more passengers getting on board.

"Squeeze in as much as you can! Passengers at the back, please squeeze in!" she heard someone shout from the door up at the far end. There was the clomp-clomp of people coming up the aisle.

"But this place is different. We don't have to squeeze in here. That's a relief."

"It'll be a much easier trip this time. This really helps."

As they spoke, they stretched out, and pretended to sleep.

"It's getting a little warm, isn't it?" she said.

"Mm. It'll be better once we take off. Maybe even a little cold."

"Even though it's so crowded in here?"

"Mm. You're right. There is quite a crowd. Nobody's sitting upright anymore. Everyone's just stuffed all over the place. Some people are even standing on the seats."

"Ah. That must be why it's so warm," she replied, her eyes still closed.

"Move down! Squeeze in!" a voice shouted from the entranceway. The next moment the name of a certain very important government official was announced, with the statement, "Make room, make room for the minister and his entourage to board the vehicle!"

"People like that do exactly as they please, without regard for anyone else," she said. Or perhaps just thought.

"The minister and his entourage will board the vehicle now!" There was a noise as a lot of shoes—presumably of the entourage—clomped up the stairs. Suddenly, she realized that the surface underneath her prone body had rucked up, like a concertina. The minister's entourage had pushed in with such a violent jolt that the passengers inside, already packed, had been shoved right to the back.

"But this is the very worst place I could be! I can't move at all!" she said. She couldn't tell if her husband was even by her side anymore. The men's backs were like a thick wall packed between her and the door, her horizontal body pinned into the angle of the windowpane, the only thing between her and the darkness outside—all at once, she couldn't breathe. When had it become night? And she thought, *So, I'm going to have to remain like this for eighteen hours? I won't be able to last even ten minutes!* She started to thrash about, and then woke up.

It was a warm night, typical of late spring, and the air was humid.

The suffocation and immobility she had just experienced had been in a vehicle in a dream, she realized, but the same sort of feeling would often overtake her in her waking life, even on overland trains. As soon as she set foot inside, she would feel confined—no seat, no matter how spacious, would be wide enough. Arriving at her destination she would feel true relief. An eighteen-hour journey would be unendurable. Was there really no way to go lying horizontally, in comfort, as she was now…?

She pondered these things for a while, listening to the even breathing of the sleeping form beside her in the darkness, who was clearly comfortable in a room where the windows were covered only by curtains, and savoring her own sense of comfort. She finally drifted off to sleep.

The sound of a heavy thud woke her. She sensed her husband was awake too. Both of them strained their ears.

"What was that?" her husband asked.

"The fence! I'm sure of it!"

"I think you're right." He got out of bed. "Turn on the light," he said. He went out onto the engawa, and pushed aside a curtain.

Just then she heard:

"Go to hell!"

"Oh, now it's over there." Her husband came back into the room then went into the hallway, out the front door, and into the road. Someone appeared to have come out of the house opposite. She heard a man's voice remonstrating, and then:

"Ah, get lost, will you! Go to hell!" The voice of the first man.

"Oh, he's part of your household?" she heard her husband ask. "I thought I heard something..." He continued, his voice loud. "Uh-oh! What a mess. So that's what it was."

"I'm so sorry. Before doing anything else..."

But now yet another neighbor seemed to have run up. "What the hell do you mean smashing our window like that? And simply leaving, without owning up?"

Her husband came hurrying back inside.

"Our gate's wrecked. One of the posts."

"One of the posts?!" she asked, standing in the hallway, wrapped in a night jacket. "Wrecked how?"

"Don't go out," he warned, seeming to catch the shrill note

in her voice. "There's a drunk." He continued: "It appears he's done damage to the house on the corner too. It's some guy from across the road."

He went into the guest room and shut the screens inside the windows. She looked at her watch. It was past one o'clock.

There was nothing to do but try to get back to sleep. She switched off the light. The voices out front continued softly for a while, then ceased.

Her husband's departure was now only three days away. The drunk had done nothing to the back fence, but it was still in a precarious state. Was her husband not going to do anything about that? He hadn't told her in any detail about how badly the gate was damaged—but if the front gate was to be mended, there was a chance he would attend to the back fence too.

There was the sound of footsteps on the road out front. The door of the house opposite opened. There was some talking, a short pause, more talking, the sound of several sets of footsteps going off into the night.

"What's happened to the gate post?"

"Stop making such a fuss. We'll talk about it tomorrow."

But it appeared this was not to be.

She was not truly asleep, but she nevertheless gave a start when the doorbell rang. About half an hour had passed. Her husband went to the front door.

"I'm sorry to bother you at such a late hour," someone said. From the polite tone, she assumed it was someone from the house opposite. But then she heard:

"Terrible behavior. In a few minutes, we'll be taking him down to the station. We'd appreciate it if you could come in too, sir, to assist in our investigation, now. The owner of the house with the smashed window is coming. I apologize for the inconvenience."

Her husband returned to the room. "I'll be away for a few hours. Can't be helped. What a night." He started to get dressed.

"And sir!" It was the voice of the police officer. His dark shape loomed from their hallway.

"Dear, I think he wants you."

"I'll be right out," her husband called, getting dressed.

"Er...merely a suggestion, sir, but perhaps bring your wife. We wouldn't want to leave her all alone at this hour after such an incident."

No doubt he'd been told to bring all potential witnesses in and was being deferential to get them to comply. Having won over the husband, he must have realized that he had to include the wife, lest she object, worried about her husband getting to work in the morning. What a thoughtful policeman.

When she'd gotten herself ready and gone out into the hallway, she saw the officer was one of the two who'd come to the house when they'd been burgled. Surely, he would remember her. The officer, however, showed no sign of it. "Much obliged," he said simply, and so she pretended she didn't know him. Had her husband done the same? Perhaps he hadn't realized.

The police officer led the way out of the house. He pointed at the gate. "What a mess," he said. One of the two tile-and-plaster posts, broken in half, lay on the ground. The black, thick-slatted gate, attached by a single hinge to the post, leaned against a shrub.

"Your car awaits," the police officer urged.

A black-and-white patrol car was parked to block the end of their little road. As they approached, the officer opened the door for them, like a chauffeur. The only difference between them and a suspect, it suddenly struck her, was that a suspect would be wearing handcuffs.

As the car turned onto the main road, she looked at the houses on both sides, strict and forbidding, all clad in armor. Each and every one of them had a parked car outside. In newspaper human-interest articles, she often came across the phrase "before dawn." It was before dawn now, which meant that they had crossed over to the next day, and her husband was leaving in not three but two days… But this was the first time she had ever ridden in a patrol car, and she kept that thought to herself.

However, the next moment, the words seemed to slip out of their own accord.

"What are you going to do about the fence?"

"I'll ask someone about it first thing tomorrow."

What would have happened if she hadn't reminded him? And when he said tomorrow, surely he meant today? But then her husband said:

"I know a guy who fixes gates like that, no problem."

"It'll cost you a lot. Please make that clear when you make a statement for the report," the police officer advised, as he ferried them away.

Contributors

Jeffrey Angles is a poet, translator, and professor at Western Michigan University. His collection of Japanese-language poetry won the Yomiuri Prize for Literature. His translations of feminist and queer writers from Japan have won numerous awards. Among his recent translations are the feminist writer Itō Hiromi's contemporary classic *The Thorn Puller*, the queer poet Takahashi Mutsuo's poetry collection *Only Yesterday*, and the science-fiction author Kayama Shigeru's 1950s novels *Godzilla* and *Godzilla Raids Again*.

Brian Bergstrom is a Montréal-based lecturer and translator. His translations have appeared in publications including *Granta*, *Aperture*, *LitHub*, *Mechademia*, *The Penguin Book of Japanese Short Stories*, and *Elemental: Earth Stories*. His translation of *Trinity, Trinity, Trinity* by Erika Kobayashi (Astra House, 2022) won the 2022 Japan-U.S. Friendship Commission (JUSFC) Prize for the Translation of Japanese Literature. His most recent translation is *Slow Down: The Degrowth Manifesto* (Astra House, 2024) by Marxist philosopher Kōhei Saitō.

Taruho Inagaki (1900–1977) was a prolific Japanese modernist writer known for his highly idiosyncratic voice and vision, which by the 1970s had gathered a cult-like following in Japan. While a young student at an international school in Kobe, he became fascinated with other cultures, aeronautics, astronomy, and attractive young men—interests that recur throughout his oeuvre. His best-known works include *One Thousand One-Second Stories* (1923), *Miroku* (1946), and *The Aesthetics of Boy-Love* (1968).

Taeko Kono (1926–2015) is one of the most significant Japanese writers in the twentieth century, whose work, often shocking and electrifying, interrogated prevailing myths and paradigms surrounding gender and sexuality in postwar Japan. She has been described as "one of the most radically talented writers of her generation" and as a "writer's writer" whose "often épater work was hailed for its spark and originality by writers as unlike her as Kenzaburo Oe and Shusaku Endo" (Eric Banks).

Margaret Mitsutani (1953–) was born in Pittsburgh, Pennsylvania, and has lived in Japan since the mid-1970s. Her first published translation was "The Empty Can," a short story by Kyoko Hayashi. In addition to Hayashi, she has translated novels by Kenzaburo Oe, Mitsuyo Kakuta, and Yoko Tawada, and the haiku of Koi Nagata.

Lucy North is a British translator of Japanese fiction and nonfiction. Her collection *Toddler Hunting and Other Stories*, ten stories by Taeko Kono written in the 1960s, first published in 1996, included now in Weidenfeld & Nicholson's list of W&N Essentials, remains the only book in English of Kono's work. Her translation of *The Woman in the Purple Skirt* by Natsuko Imamura won the 2022 Lindsley and Masao Miyoshi Translation Prize, and her most recent publication is a collection of stories by Imamura titled *ASA: The Girl Who Turned into a Pair of Chopsticks*.

Philip Price was born in the northeast of England; studied Russian and German at the University of Glasgow; and then moved to Tokyo, where he now works full time as a Japanese-English and Georgian-English translator. His translations of Japanese and Georgian literature have appeared in various media, including the short-story collections *Inside and Other Short Fiction* and *The Book of Tbilisi*.

Nobuko Takagi is well known for works of a sensuous nature, in particular her book *Translucent Tree*, a story of love between an older couple. She traveled all over Asia and wrote a collection of stories inspired by her experiences as part of her "Soaked in Asia Project" at Kyushu University. "The Hole in the Sky" was one of those stories. Her story "Tomosui" (*Two Lines* Issue 24) received the Kawabata Yasunari Award in 2010.

Takako Takahashi (1932–2013) only began writing at the age of thirty-nine, following the death of her husband, the author Kazumi Takahashi. She converted to Catholicism in 1975, spending time in a Japanese convent and later living modestly in Paris. Her work is deeply engaged with existentialism, sexuality, and sin and is often dreamlike and disturbing, blurring the line between perception and hallucination. She won numerous major literary awards, including the Female Writers' Award, the Yomiuri Prize, and the Mainichi Arts Award.

Tomoko Yoshida (1934–) was born in Shizuoka Prefecture, Japan, but spent most of her childhood in China. After WWII, she and her mother relocated to Sakhalin for a year, returning to Japan in 1947. Her first stories were published in *Gomu*, a little magazine she started with her husband, also a writer, in 1963. Known for her unique blending of the everyday with the surreal, she has been awarded many literary prizes in Japan.

OTHER TITLES IN THE CALICO SERIES

That We May Live: Speculative Chinese Fiction

Home: Arabic Poems

Elemental: Earth Stories

Cuír: Queer Brazil

This Is Us Losing Count: Eight Russian Poets

Visible: Text + Image

No Edges: Swahili Stories

Elektrik: Caribbean Writing

Through the Night Like a Snake: Latin American Horror Stories

Cigarettes Until Tomorrow: Romanian Poetry

CALICO

The Calico Series, published biannually by Two Lines Press, captures vanguard works of translated literature in stylish, collectible editions. Each Calico is a vibrant snapshot that explores one aspect of our present moment, offering the voices of previously inaccessible, highly innovative writers from around the world today.